EDUCATION LIBRARY
UNIVERSITY OF KENTUCKY

J 398.209
ATW

How Raven Got His Crooked Nose

An Alaskan Dena'ina Fable

Retold by
Barbara J. Atwater and Ethan J. Atwater

Illustrated by Mindy Dwyer

ALASKA
NORTHWEST
BOOKS®

"Slow down, child," said Grandmother. "It is better to take your time and do things right. Do you know the story of how *Chulyen* the raven got his crooked nose?"

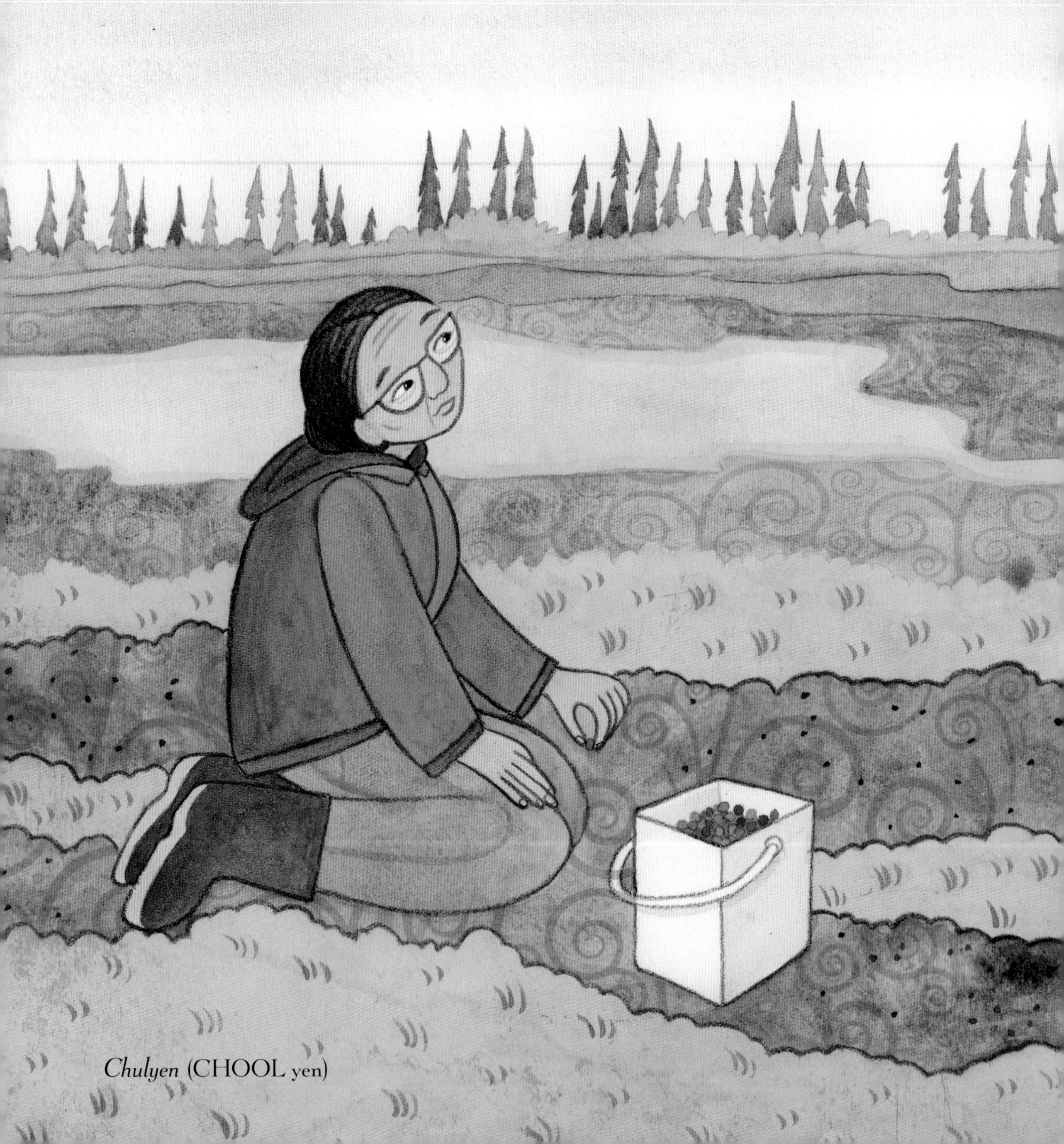

Chulyen (CHOOL yen)

Granddaughter shook her head.

"No? Then sit and I will tell you a *sukdu*."

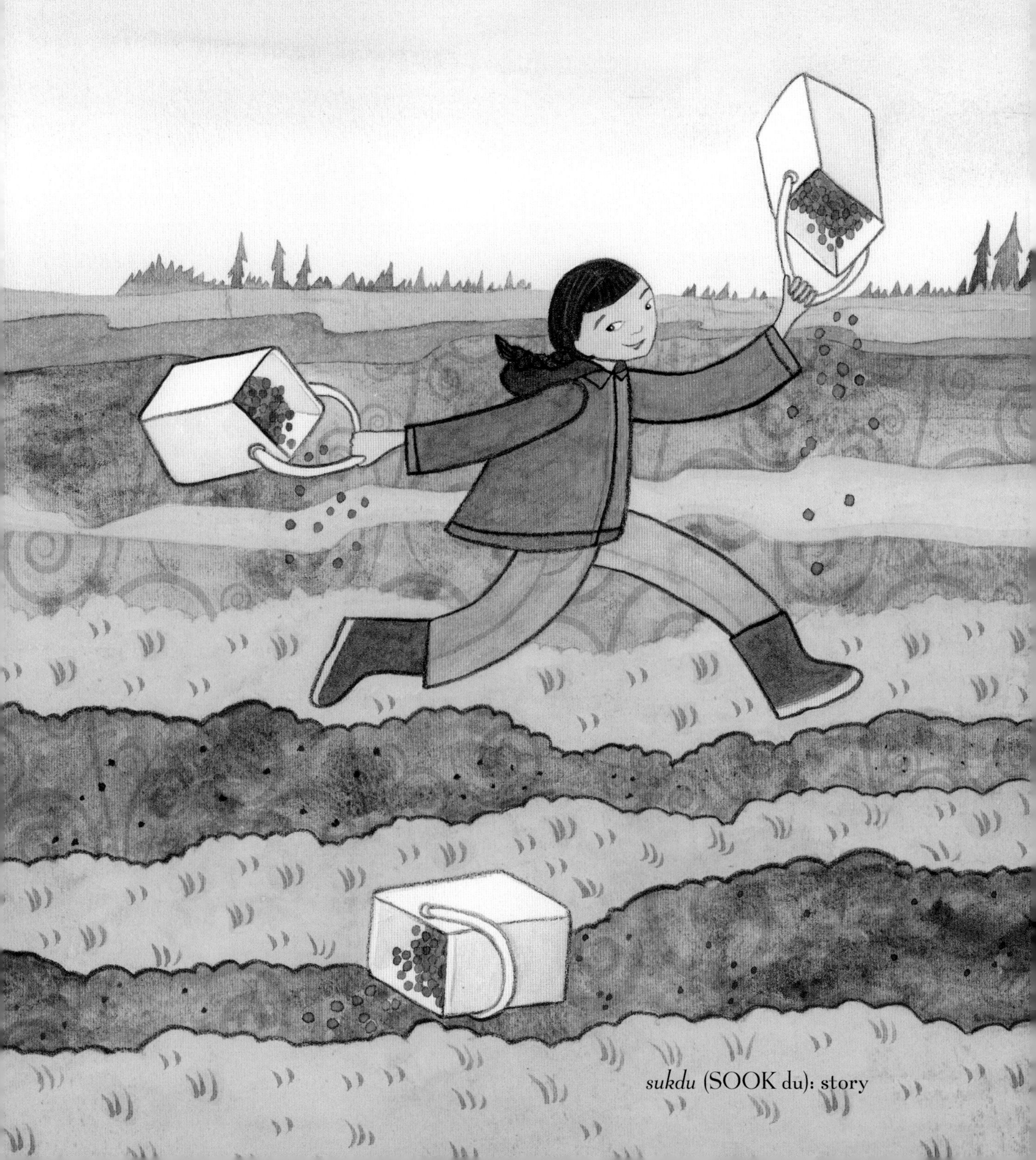

sukdu (SOOK du): story

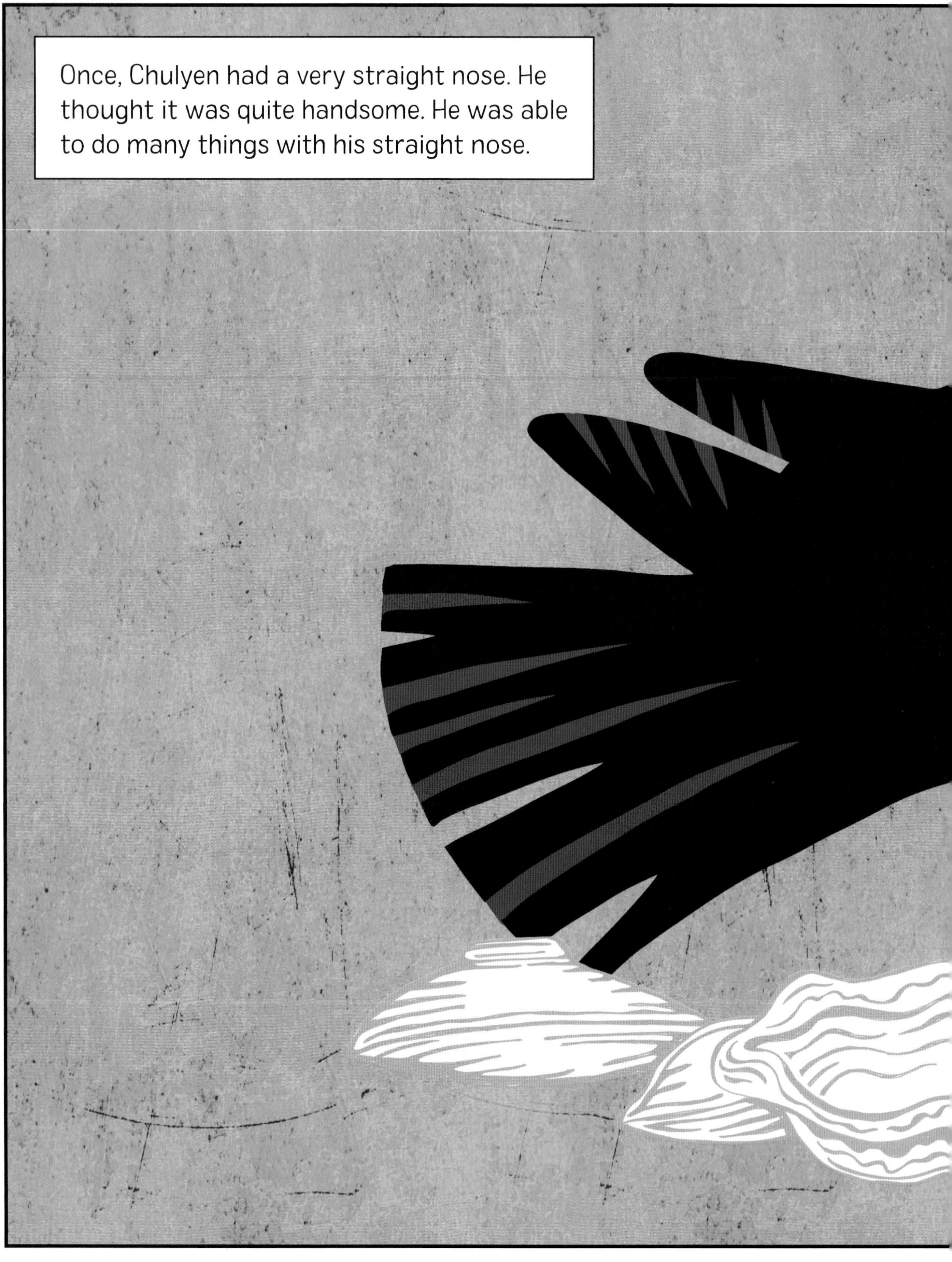
Once, Chulyen had a very straight nose. He thought it was quite handsome. He was able to do many things with his straight nose.

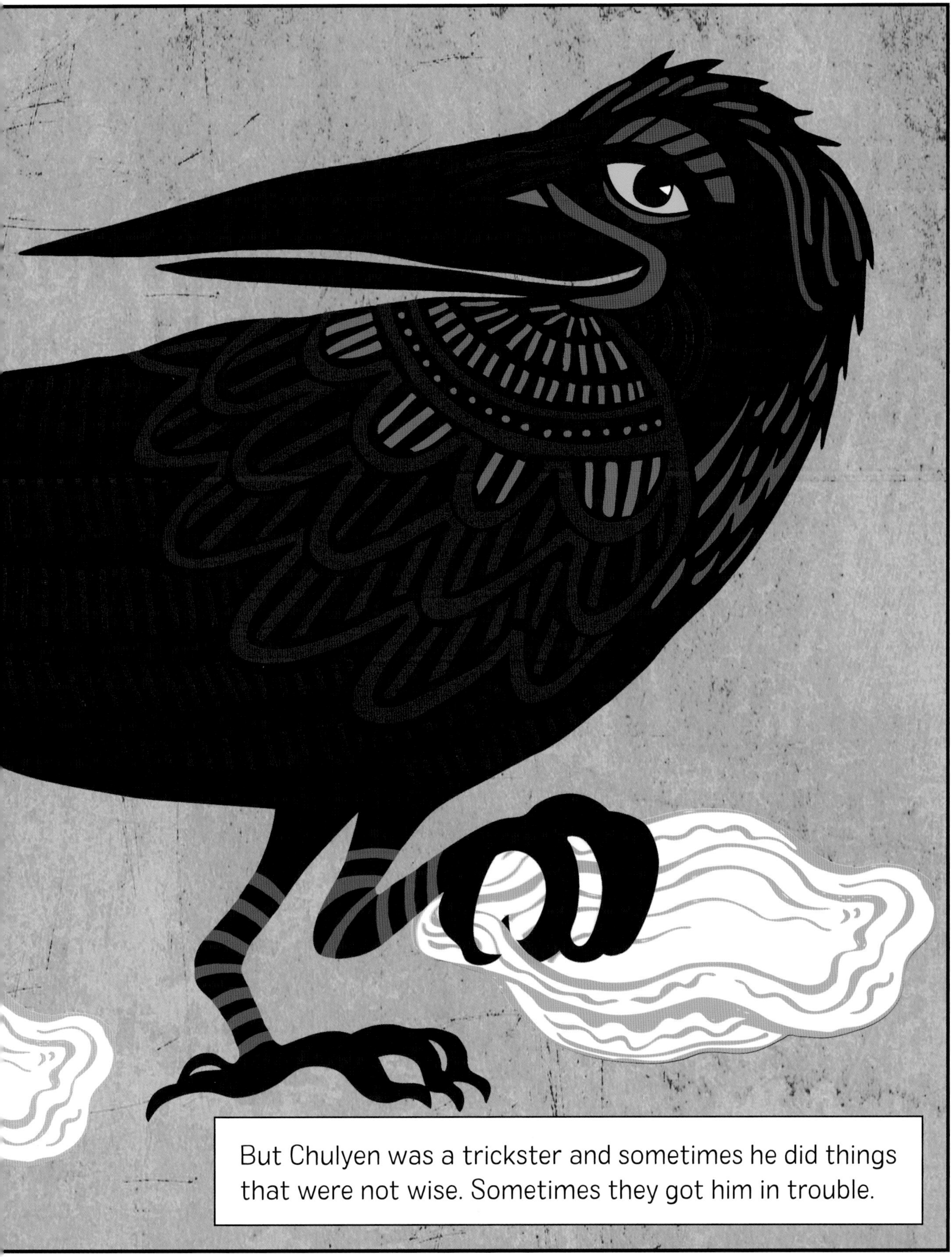

But Chulyen was a trickster and sometimes he did things that were not wise. Sometimes they got him in trouble.

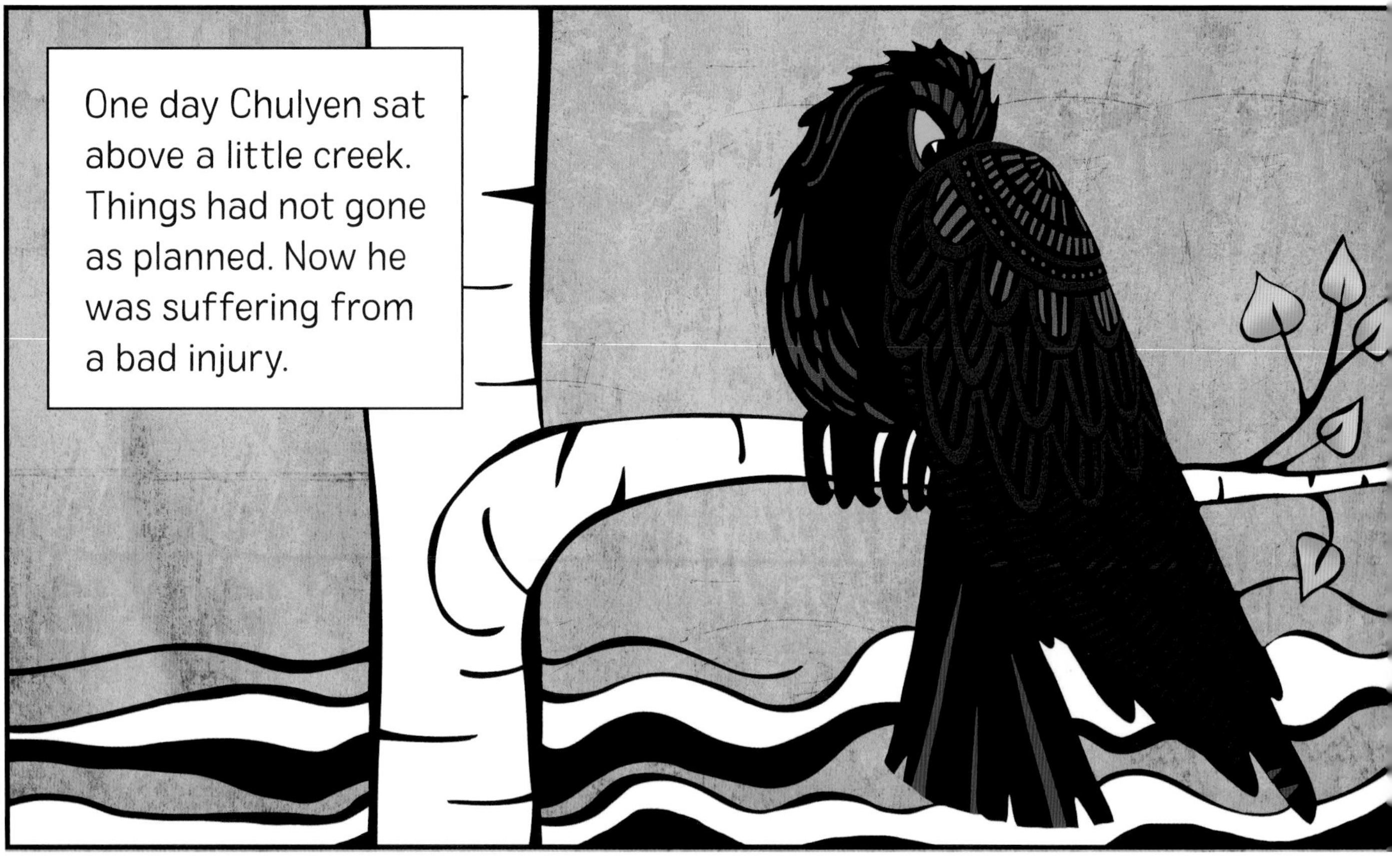
One day Chulyen sat above a little creek. Things had not gone as planned. Now he was suffering from a bad injury.

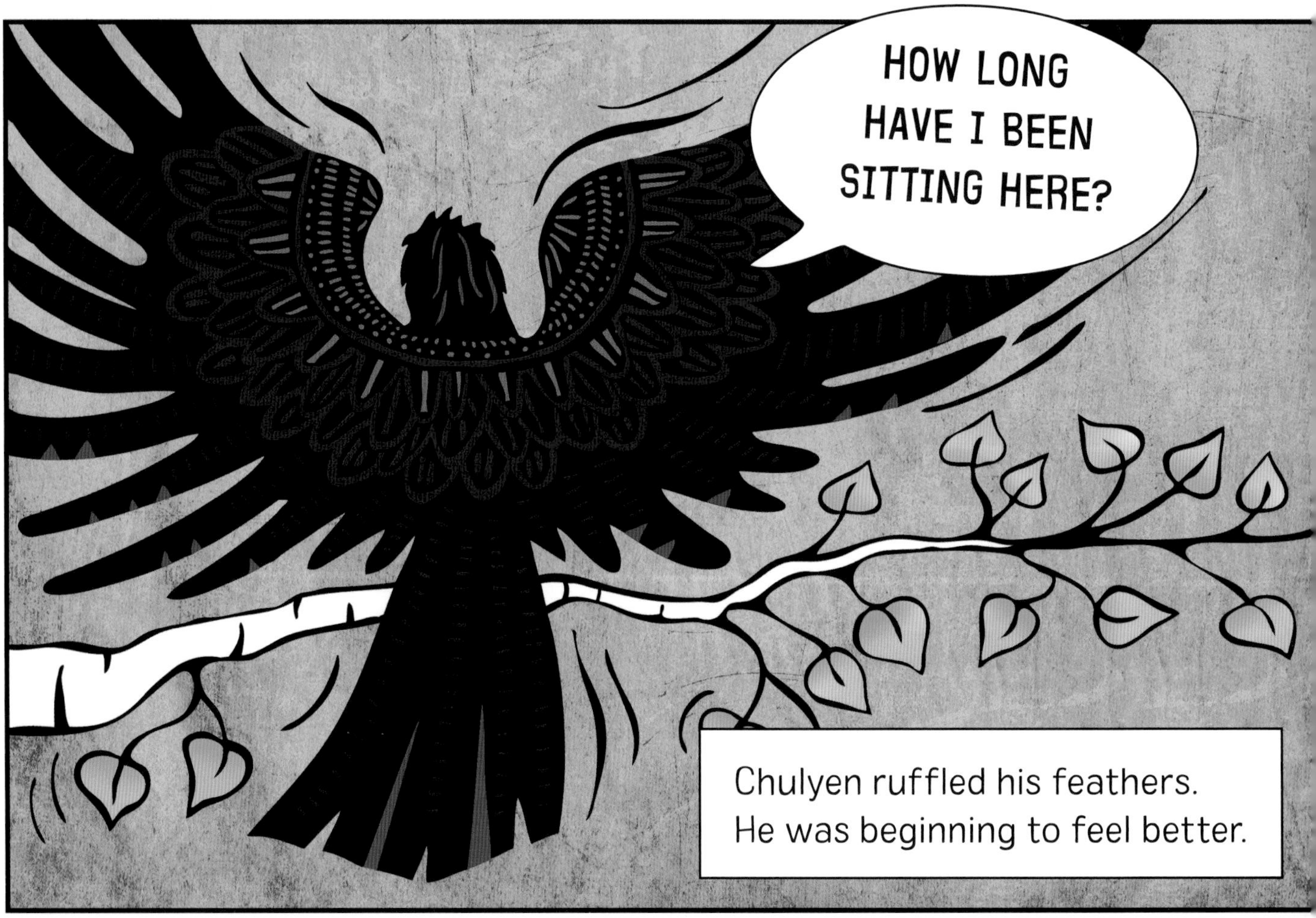
HOW LONG HAVE I BEEN SITTING HERE?
Chulyen ruffled his feathers. He was beginning to feel better.

Then Chulyen remembered...

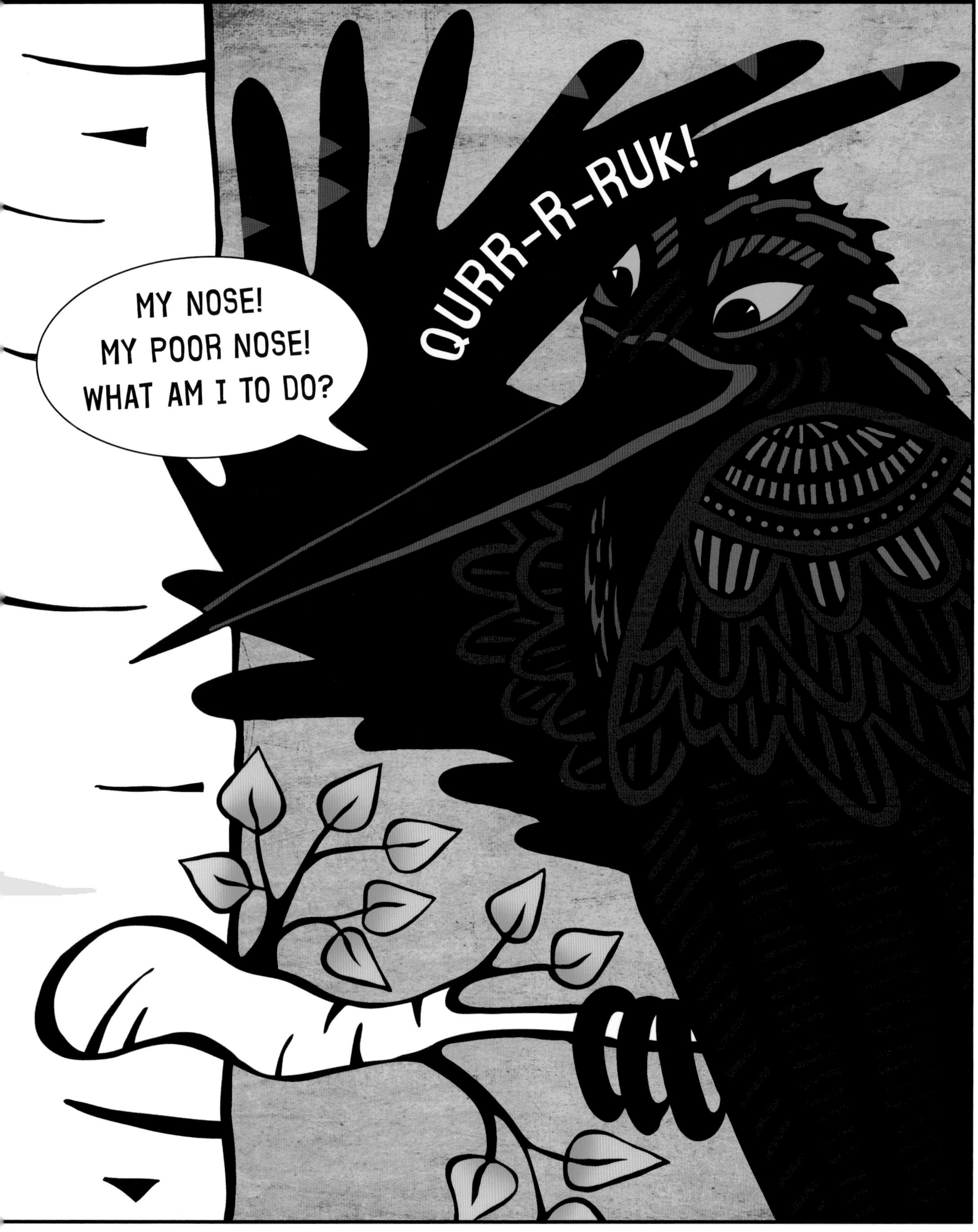
QURR-R-RUK!
MY NOSE! MY POOR NOSE! WHAT AM I TO DO?

"But how did Chulyen lose his nose?" asked Granddaughter.

"He would never say, my dear. Maybe he was too embarrassed," answered Grandmother.

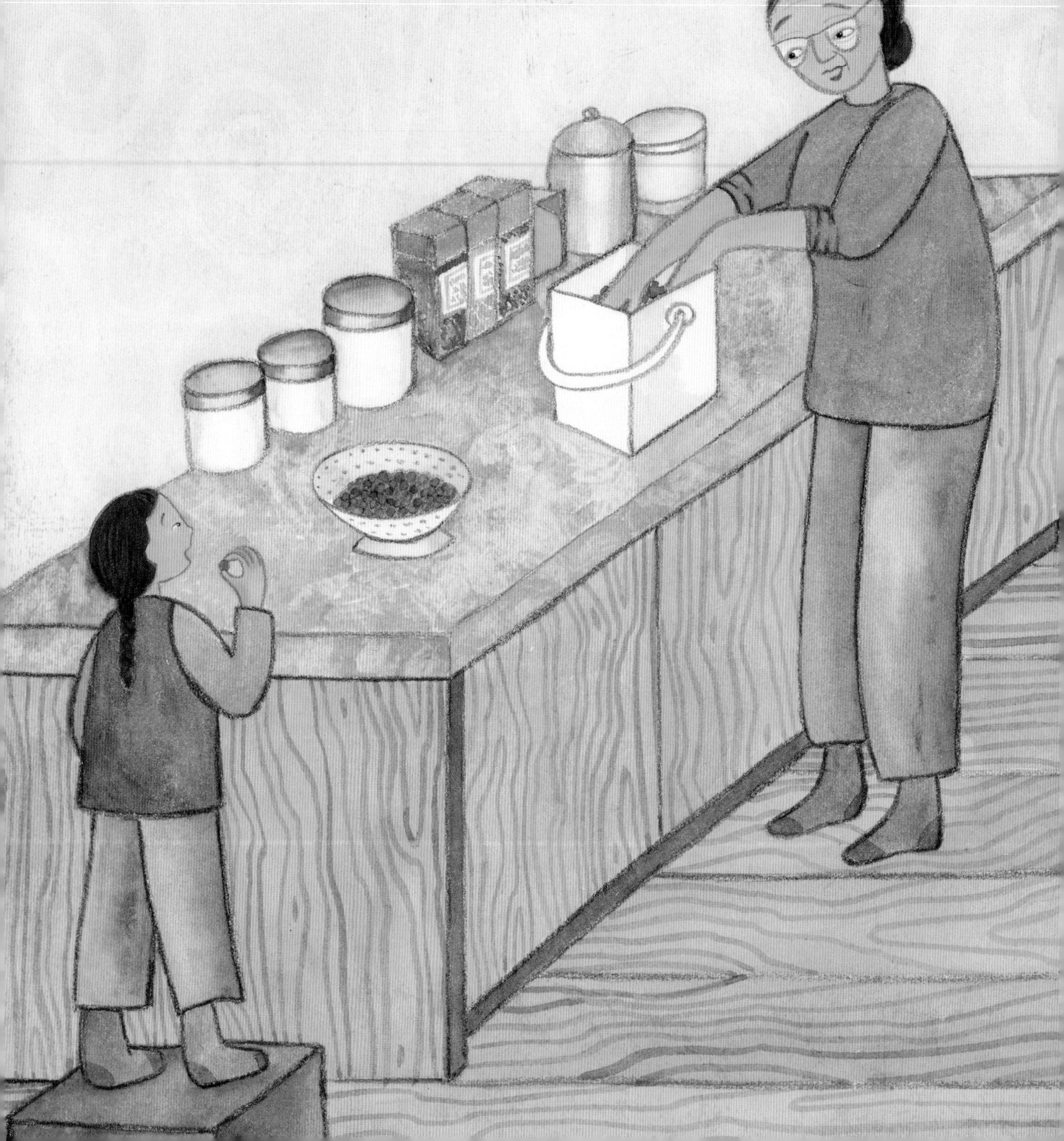

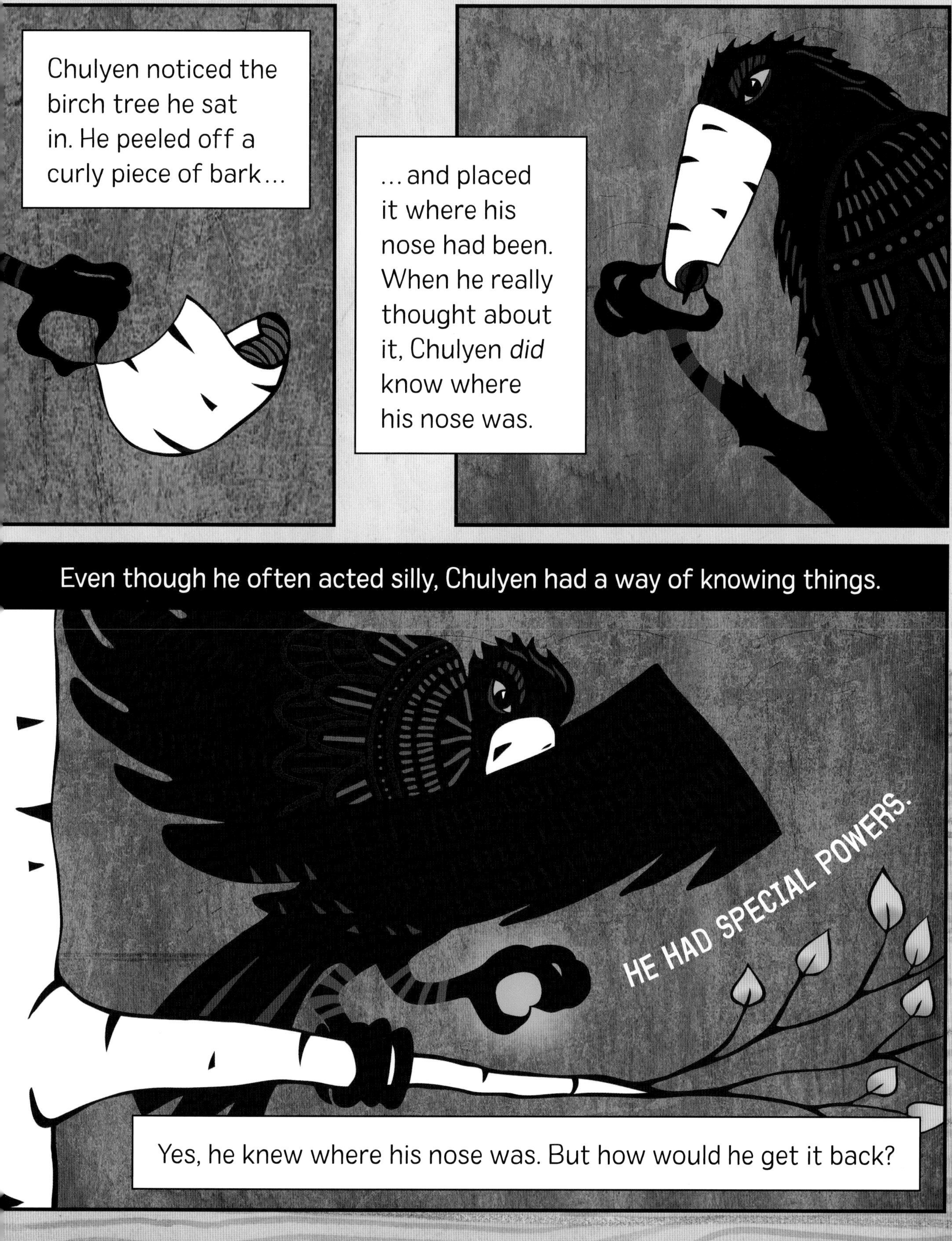
Chulyen noticed the birch tree he sat in. He peeled off a curly piece of bark…
…and placed it where his nose had been. When he really thought about it, Chulyen *did* know where his nose was.
Even though he often acted silly, Chulyen had a way of knowing things.
HE HAD SPECIAL POWERS.
Yes, he knew where his nose was. But how would he get it back?

The bubbling creek below Chulyen flowed into a lake. A small village was nestled on the hillside above it.

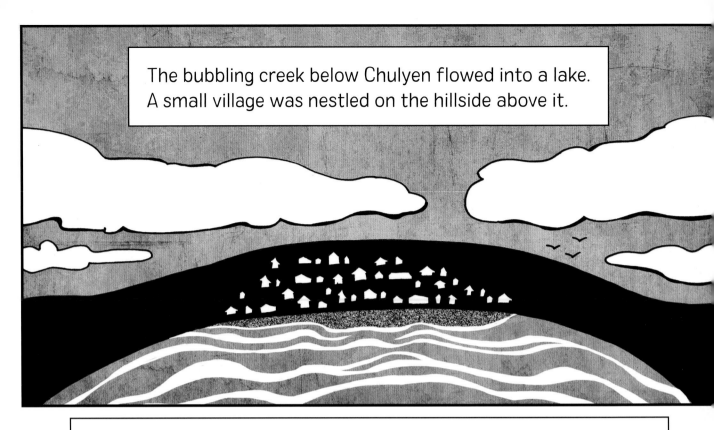

While Chulyen was thinking, a *Chida* from the village walked to the beach to gather driftwood for her fire. As she reached for a piece of wood, she noticed something.

Chida (CHEE da): old woman

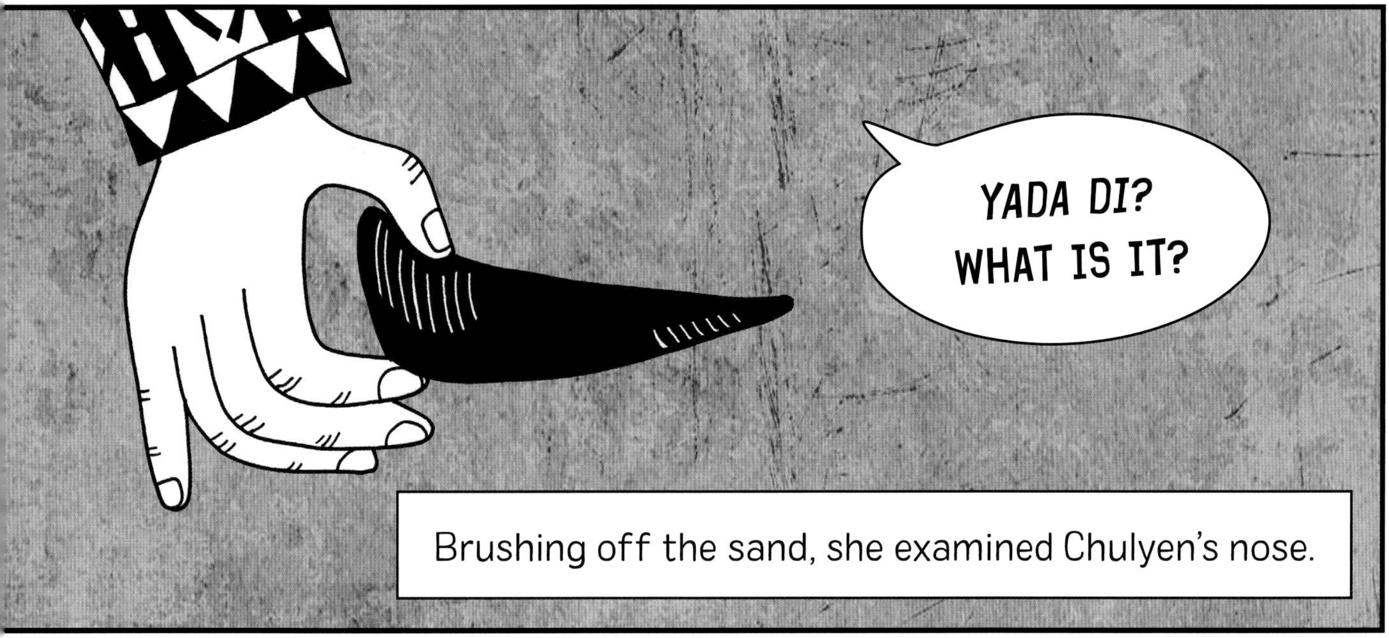
YADA DI? WHAT IS IT?
Brushing off the sand, she examined Chulyen's nose.

Yada di (ya da DEE)

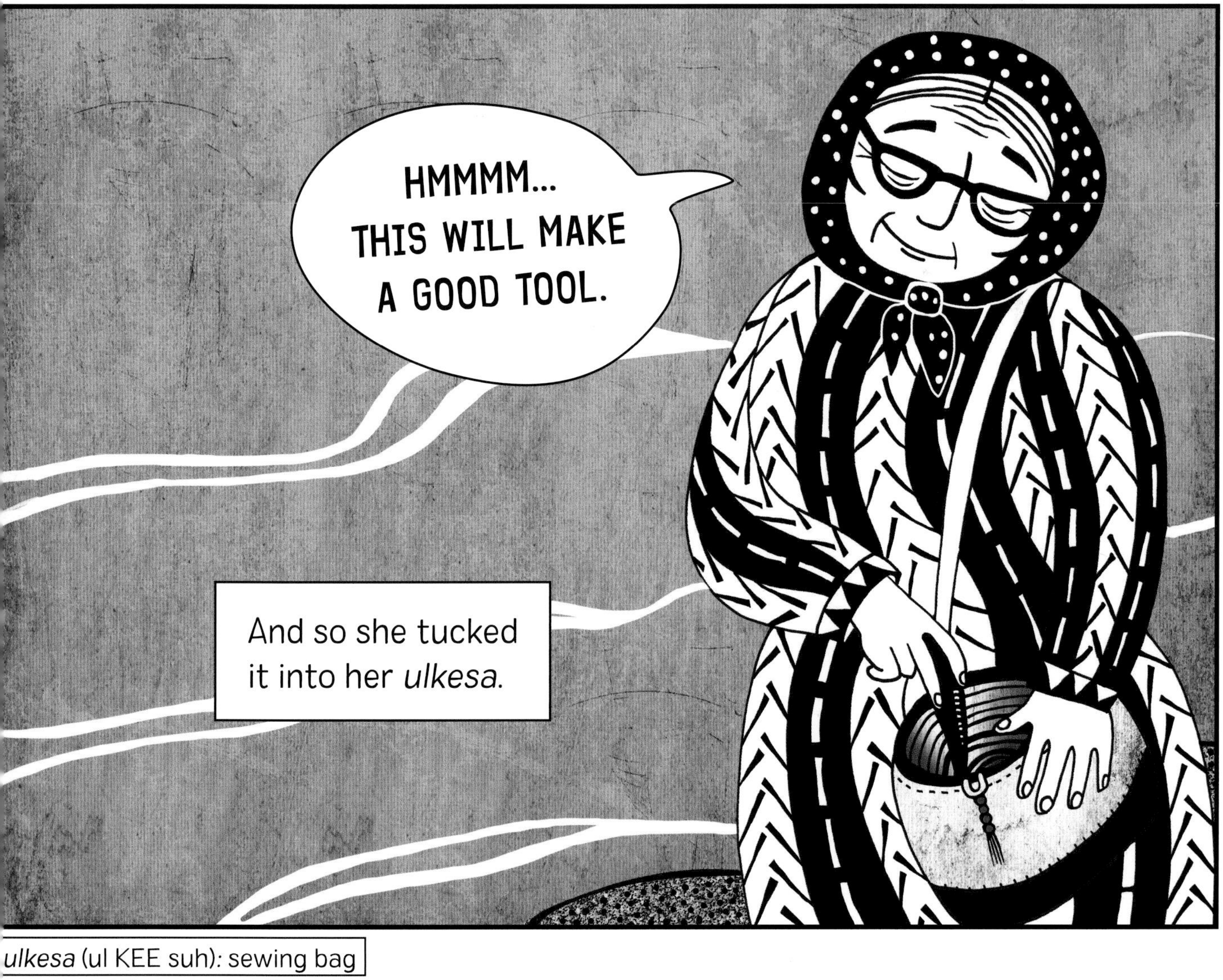
HMMMM... THIS WILL MAKE A GOOD TOOL.
And so she tucked it into her *ulkesa*.

ulkesa (ul KEE suh): sewing bag

Chida found Chulyen's nose useful for many things...

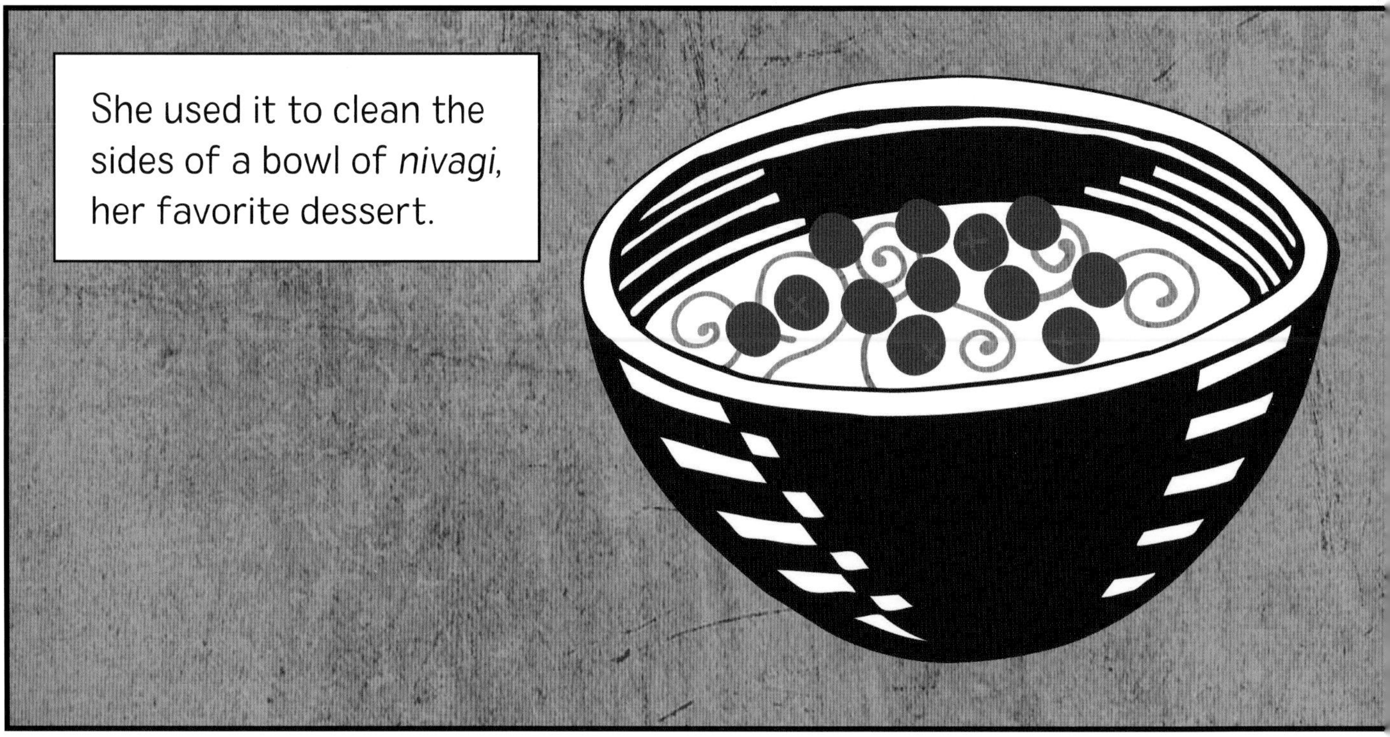
She used it to clean the sides of a bowl of *nivagi*, her favorite dessert.

nivagi (ni VAH gi)

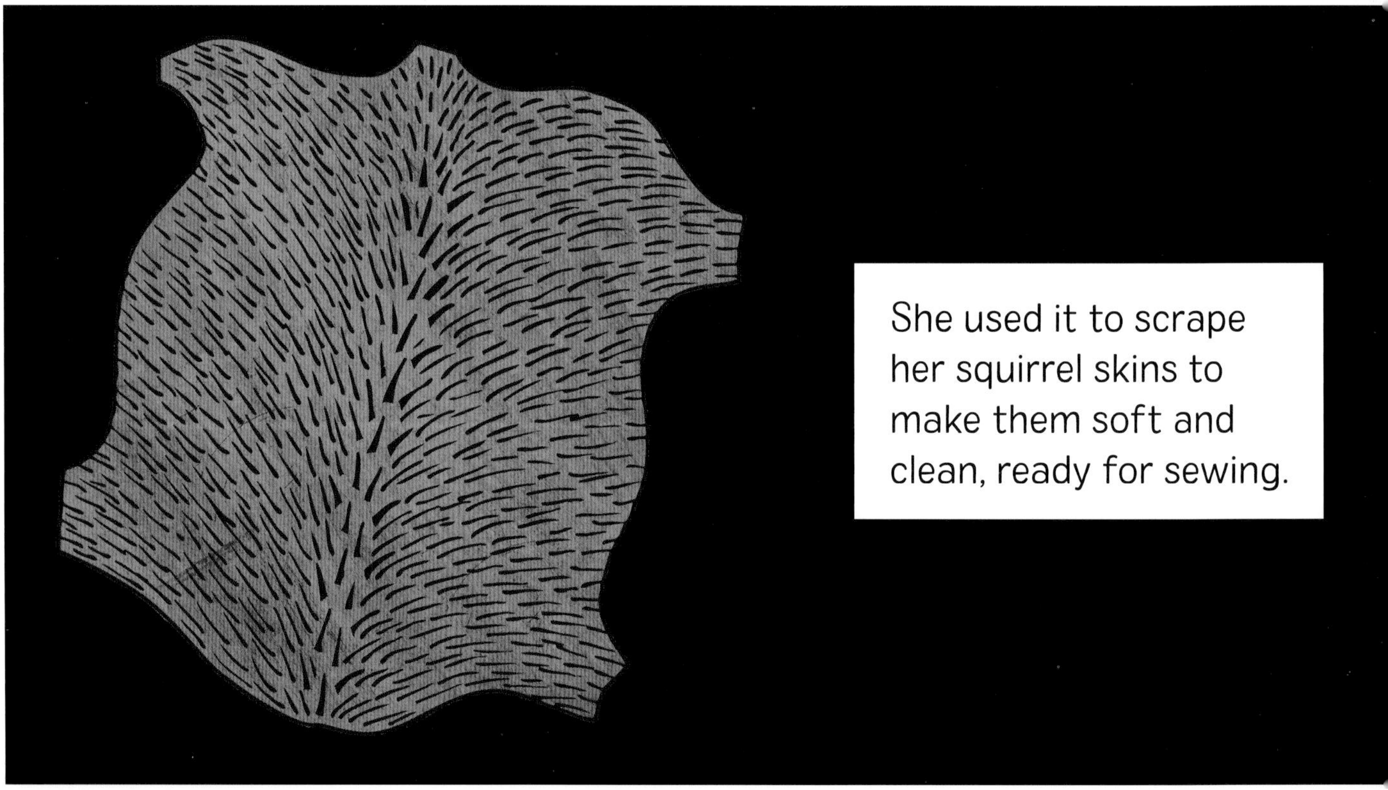
She used it to scrape her squirrel skins to make them soft and clean, ready for sewing.

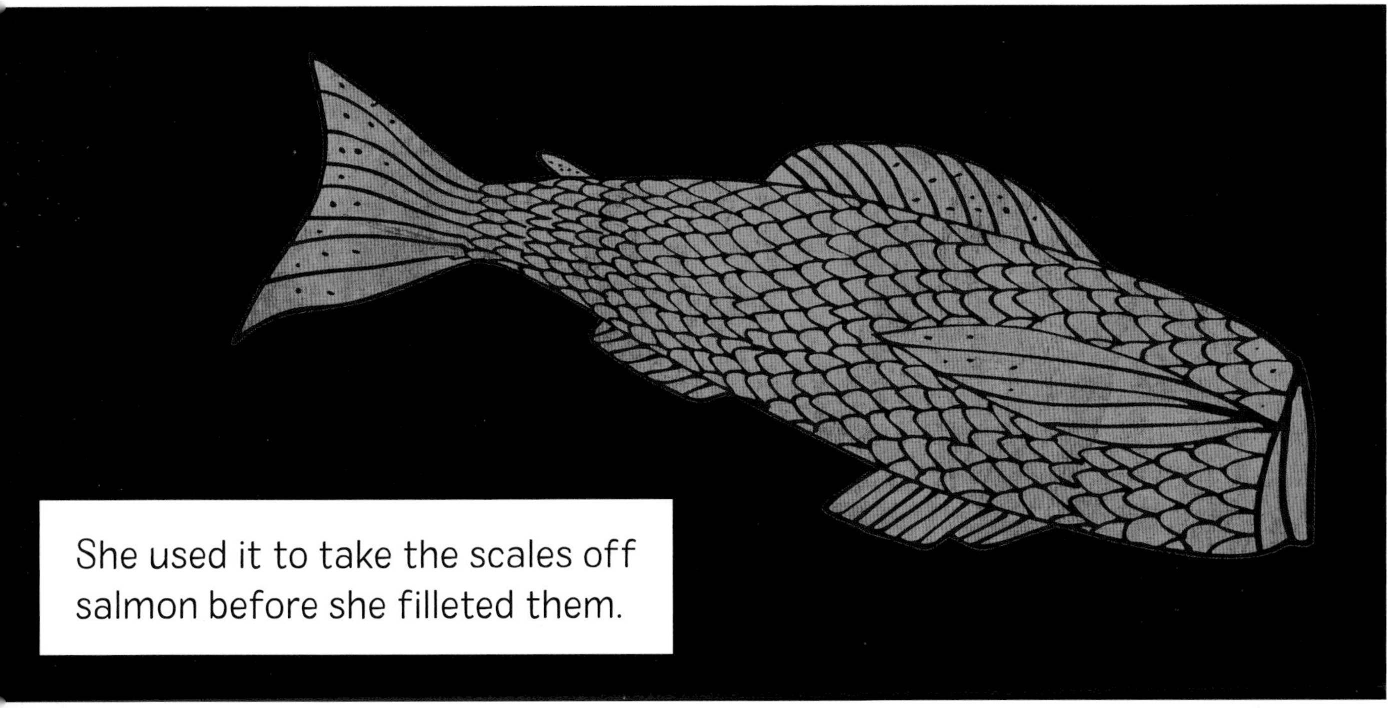
She used it to take the scales off salmon before she filleted them.

Yes, Chulyen's nose was a wonderful tool.

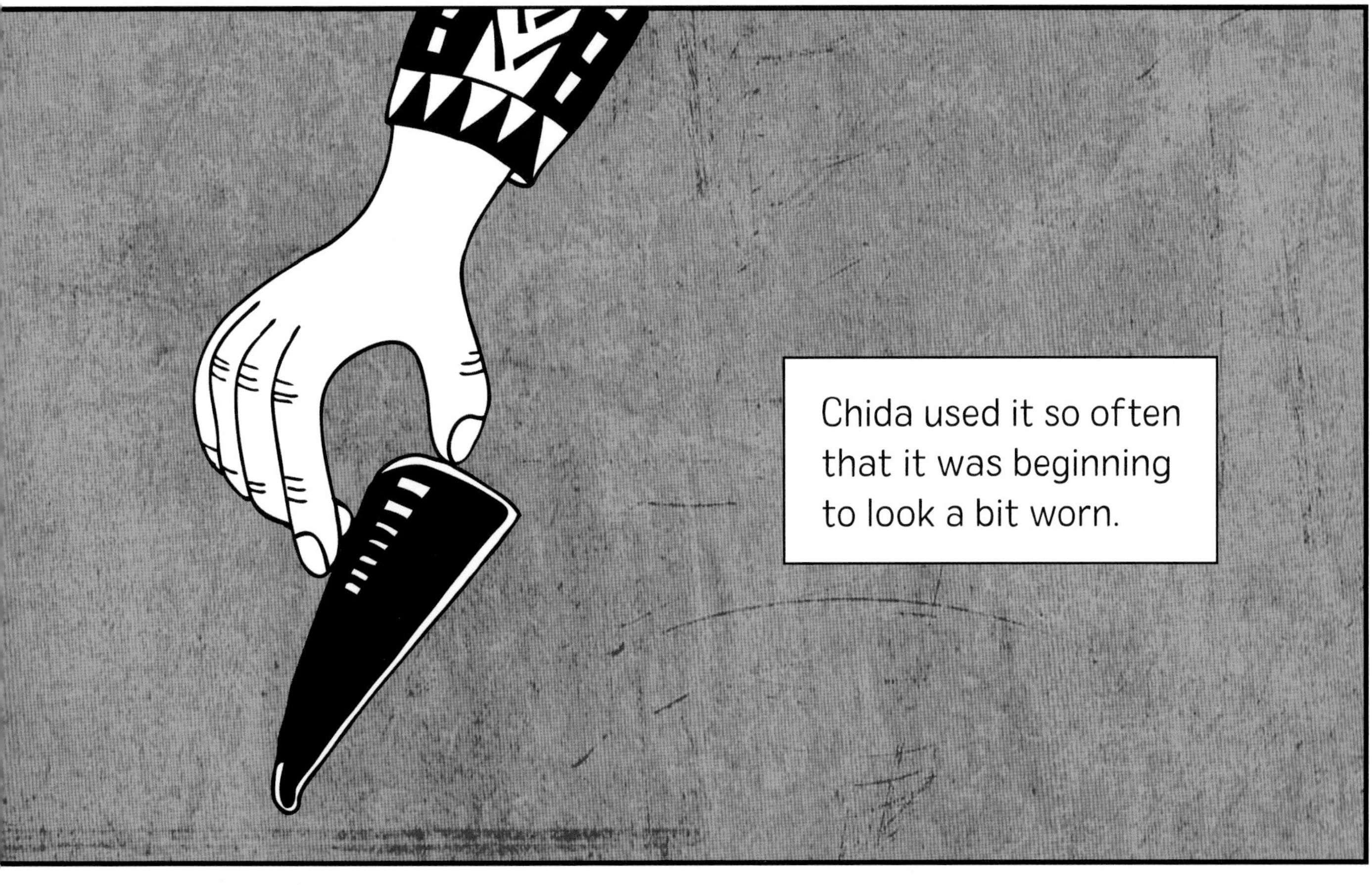
Chida used it so often that it was beginning to look a bit worn.

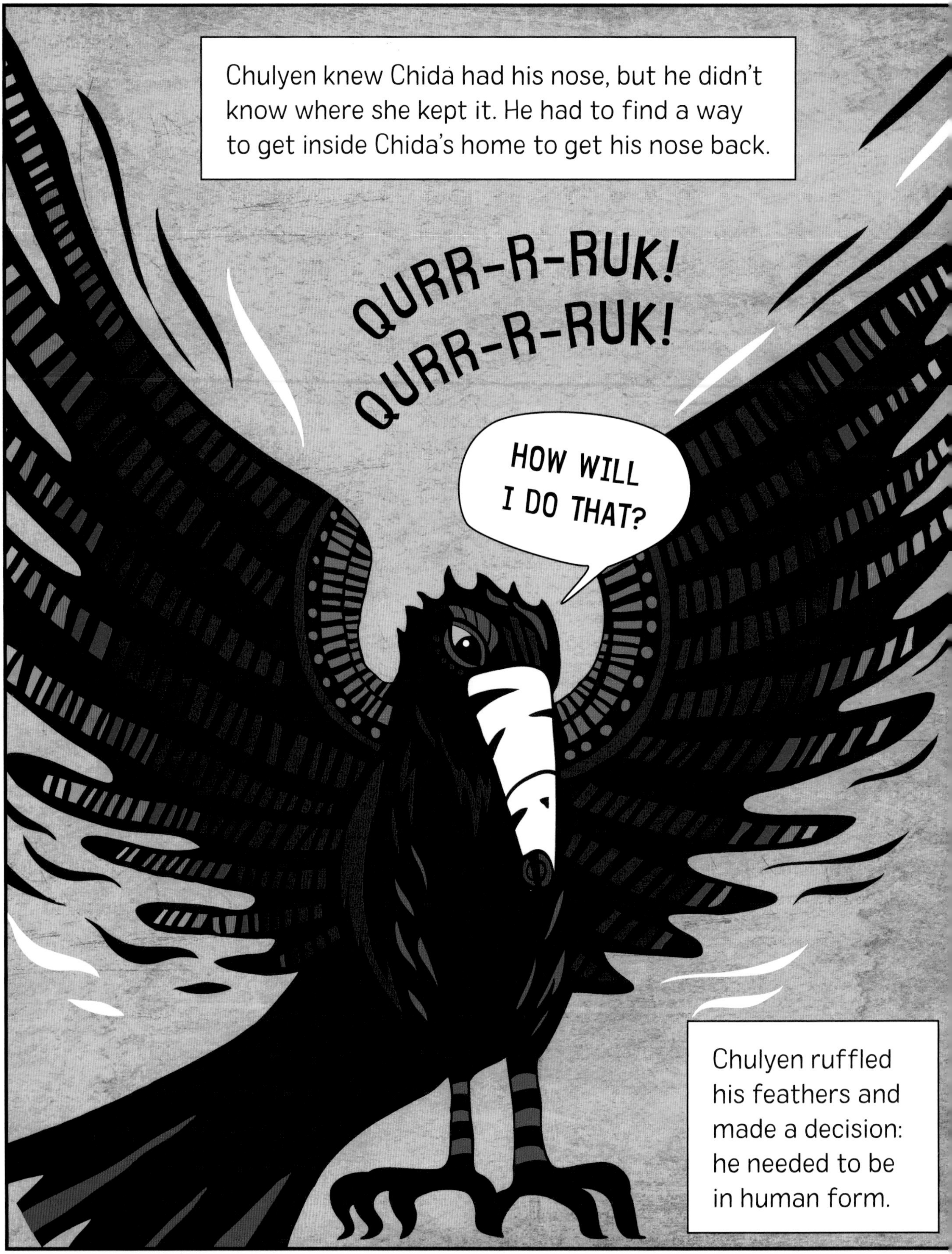
Chulyen knew Chida had his nose, but he didn't know where she kept it. He had to find a way to get inside Chida's home to get his nose back.
QURR-R-RUK!
QURR-R-RUK!
HOW WILL I DO THAT?
Chulyen ruffled his feathers and made a decision: he needed to be in human form.

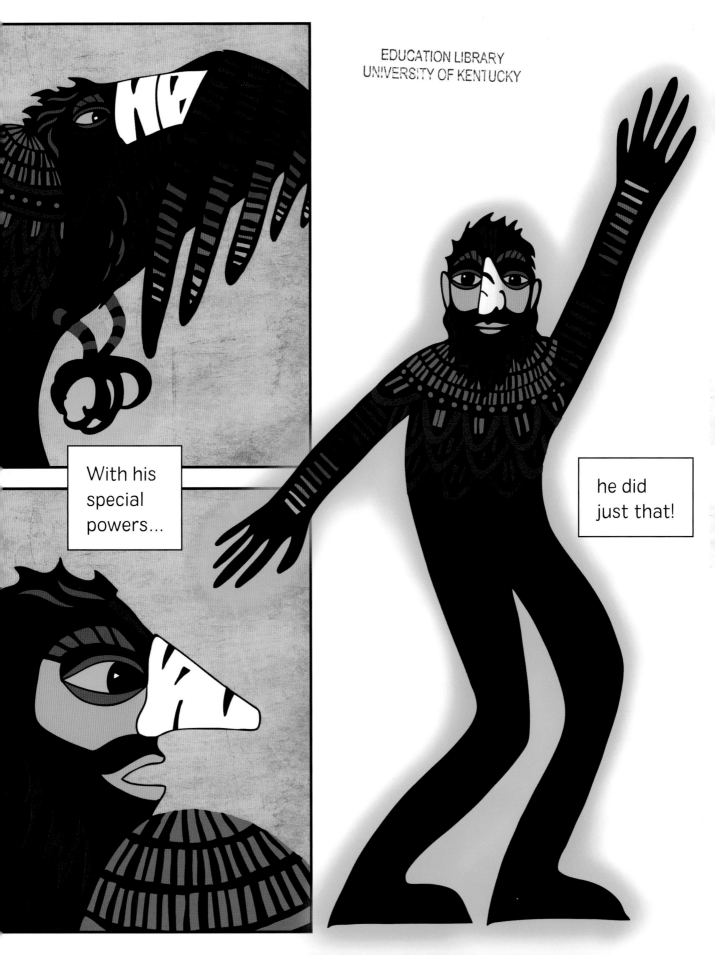

EDUCATION LIBRARY
UNIVERSITY OF KENTUCKY

"What else can Chulyen do?" asked Granddaughter.

"You will see," said Grandmother.

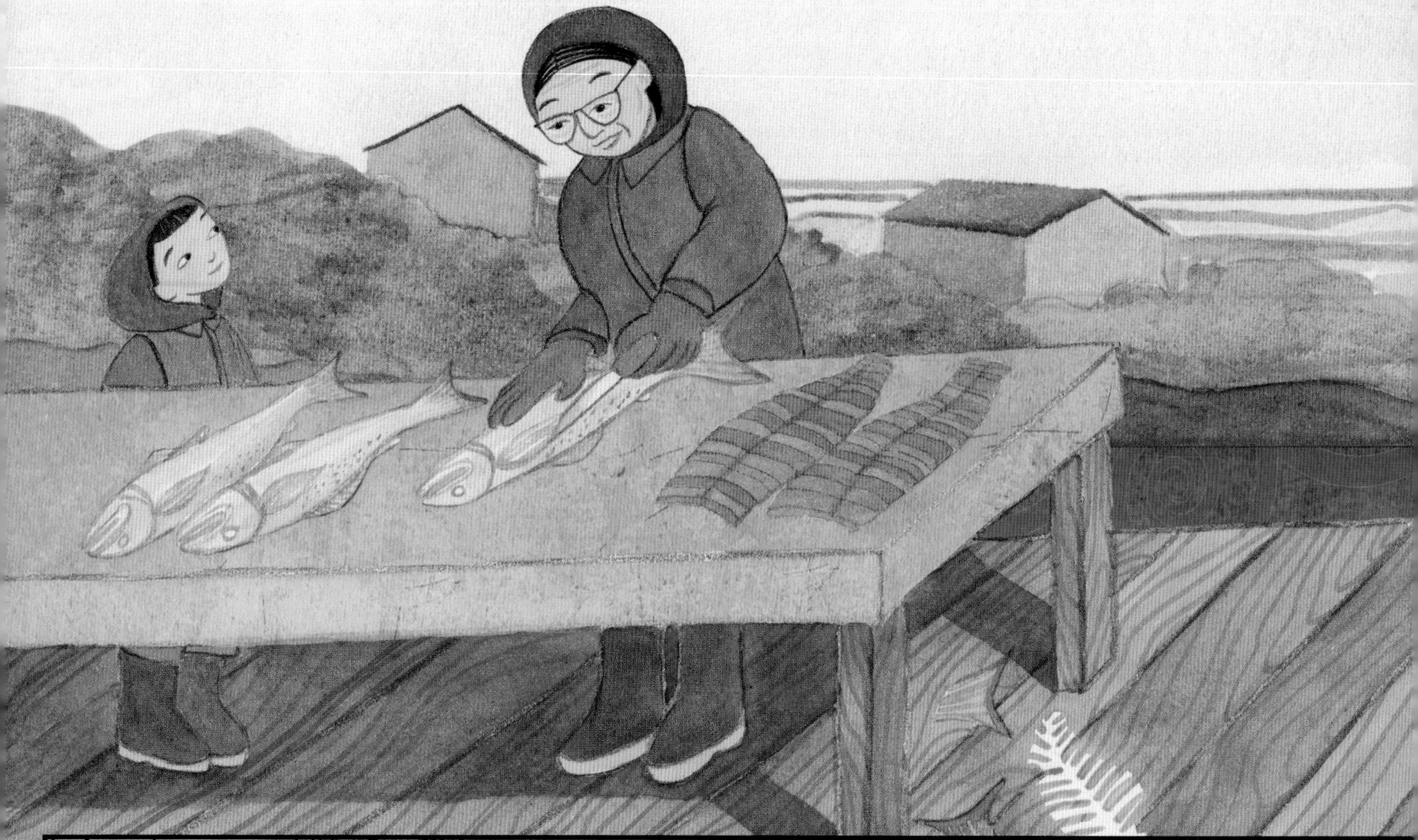

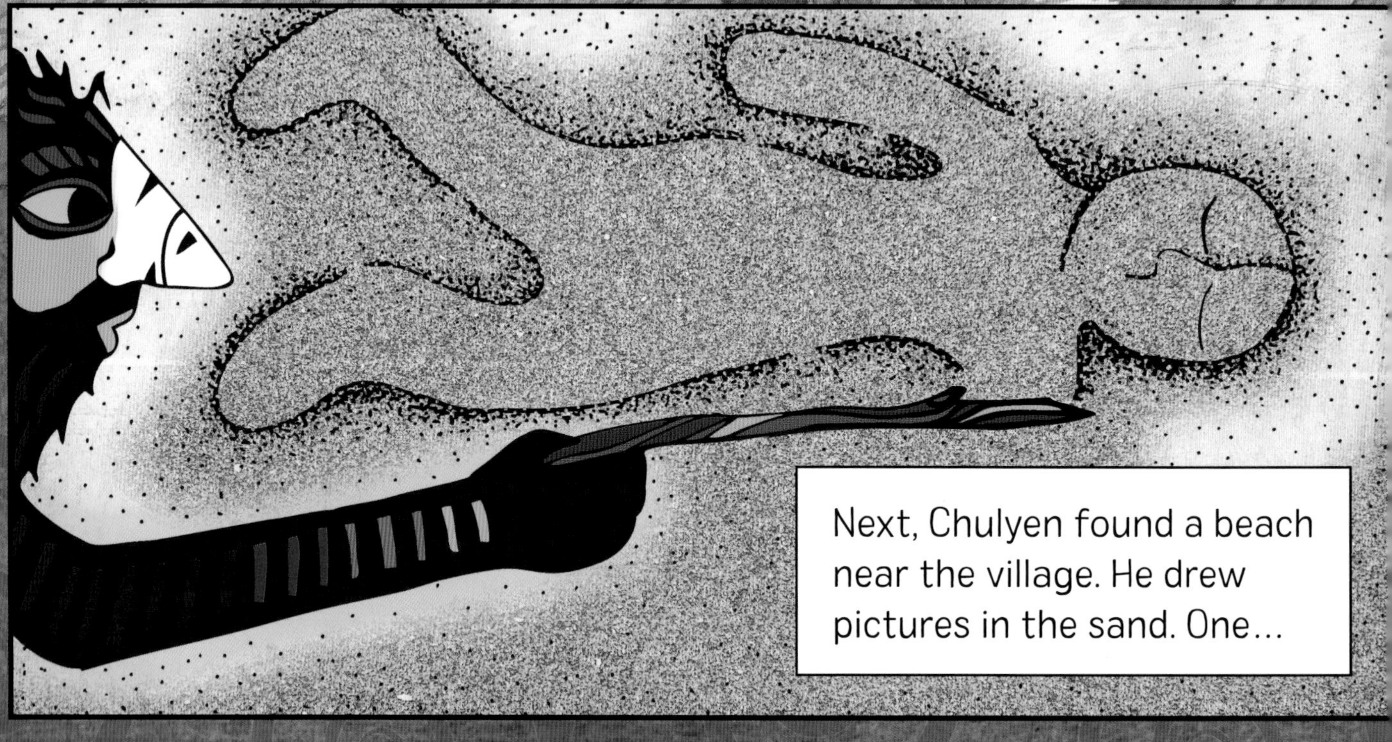
Next, Chulyen found a beach near the village. He drew pictures in the sand. One...

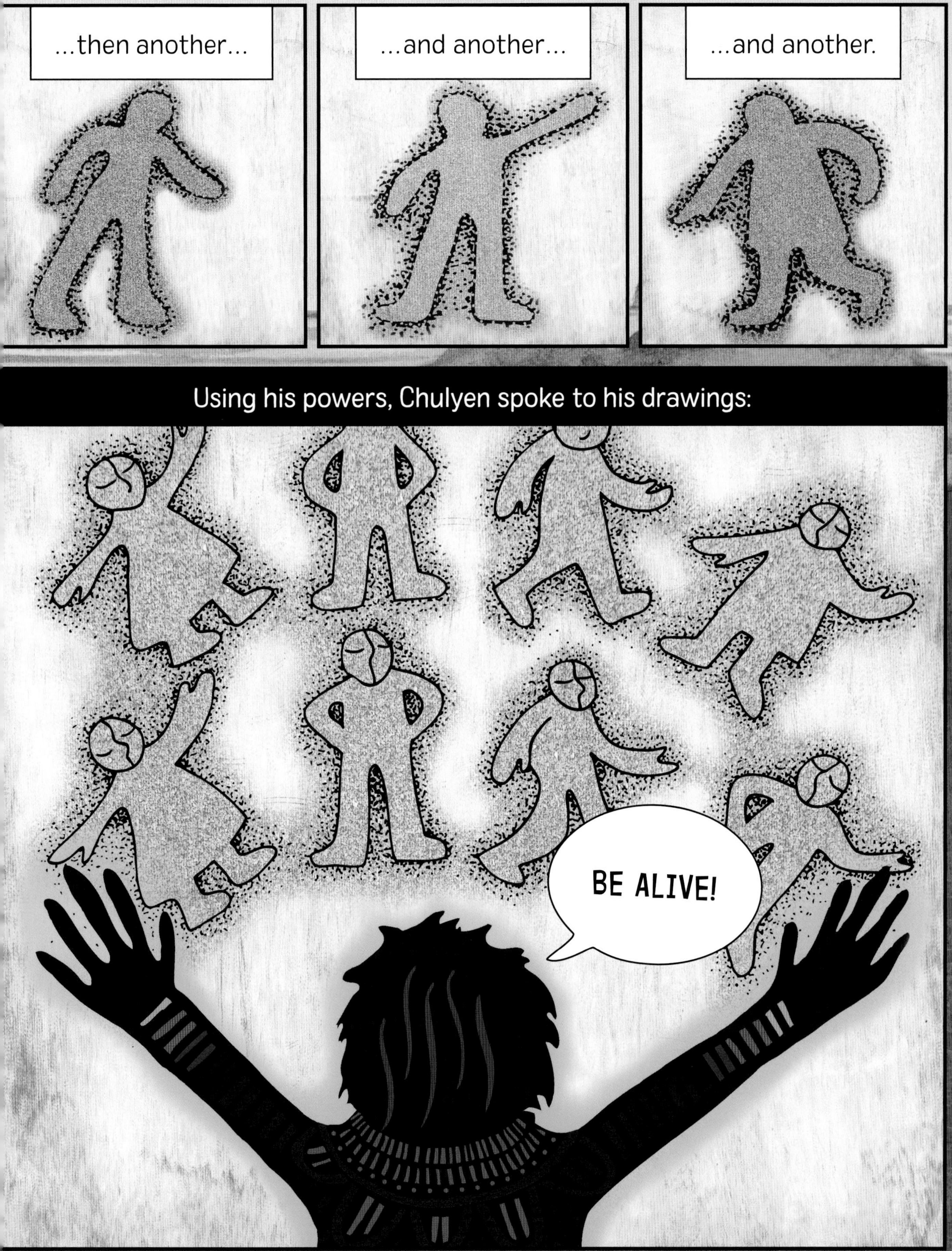
...then another...
...and another...
...and another.
Using his powers, Chulyen spoke to his drawings:
BE ALIVE!

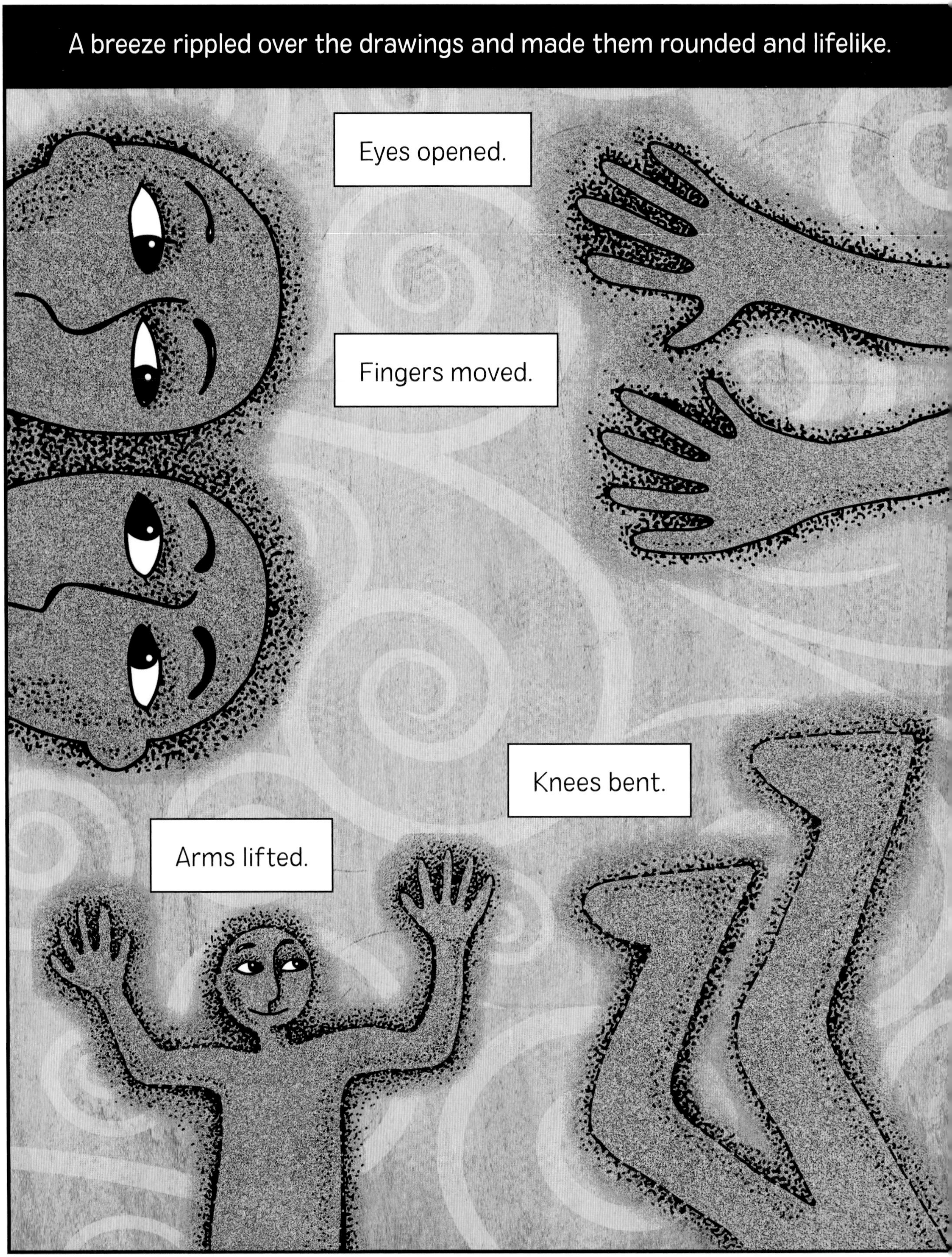
A breeze rippled over the drawings and made them rounded and lifelike.
Eyes opened.
Fingers moved.
Knees bent.
Arms lifted.

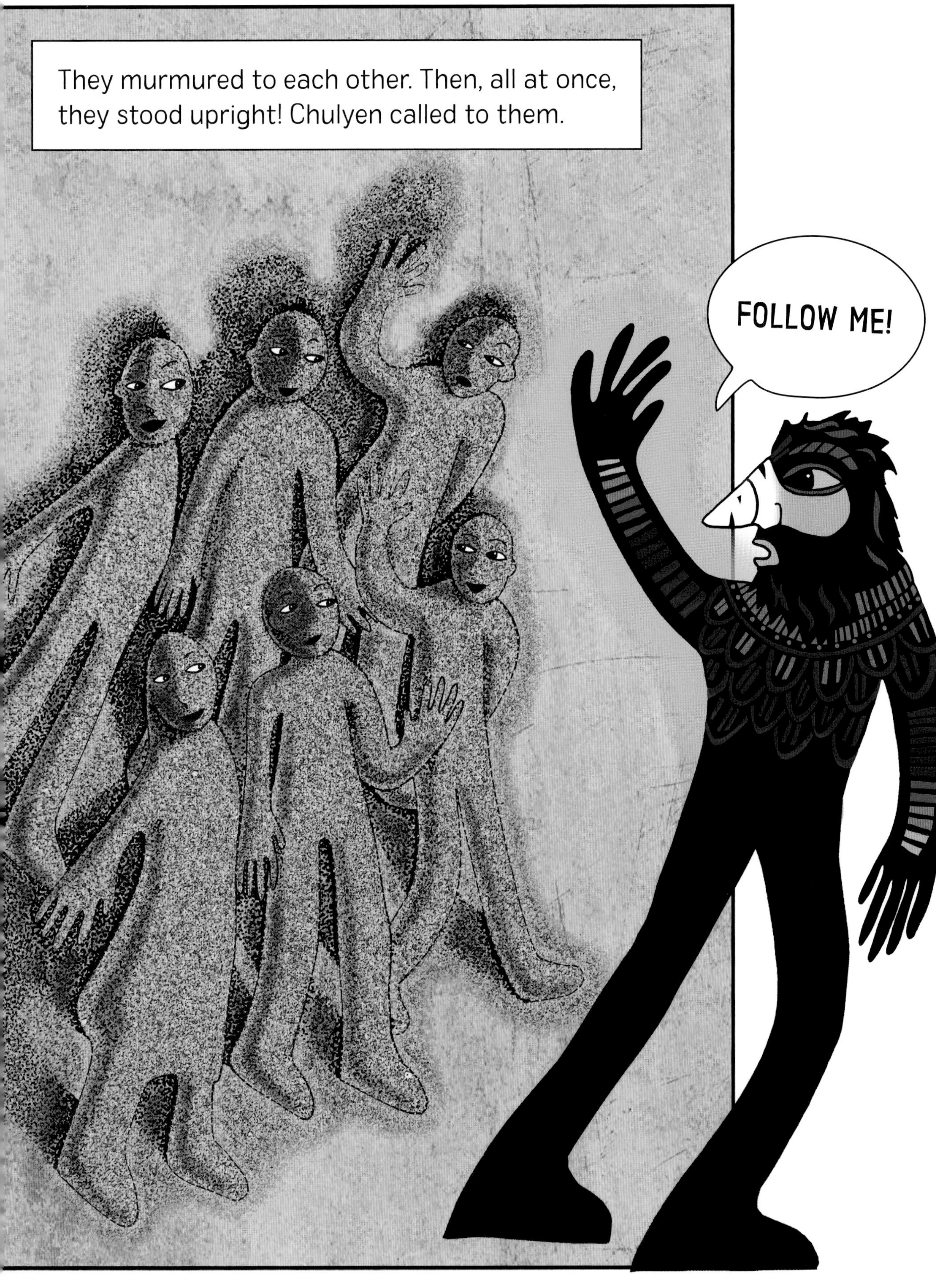
They murmured to each other. Then, all at once, they stood upright! Chulyen called to them.
FOLLOW ME!

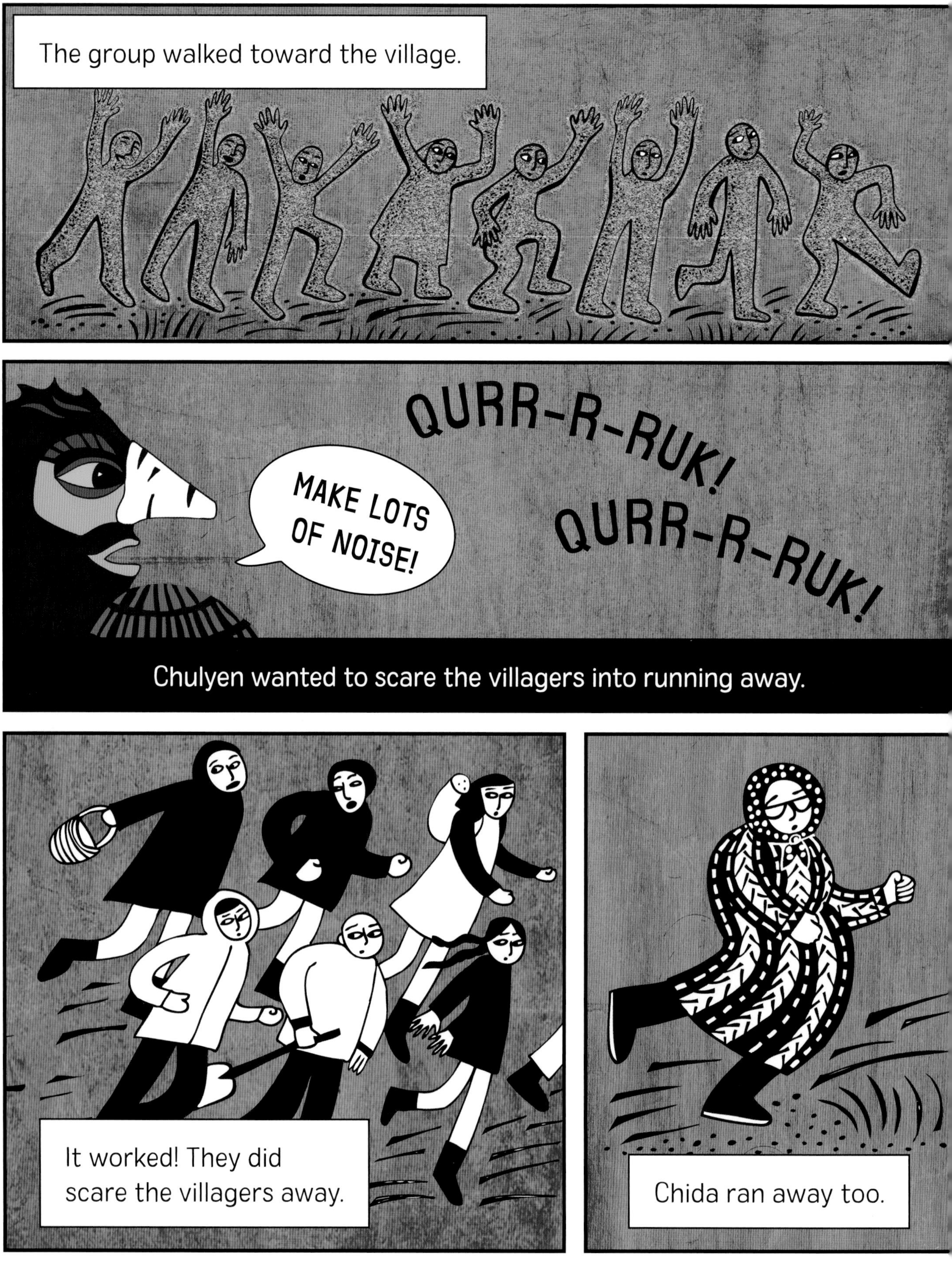
The group walked toward the village.
MAKE LOTS OF NOISE!
QURR-R-RUK! QURR-R-RUK!
Chulyen wanted to scare the villagers into running away.
It worked! They did scare the villagers away.
Chida ran away too.

Chulyen knew he did not have much time, for his magic did not last long. His sand drawings would disappear soon and the villagers would return.

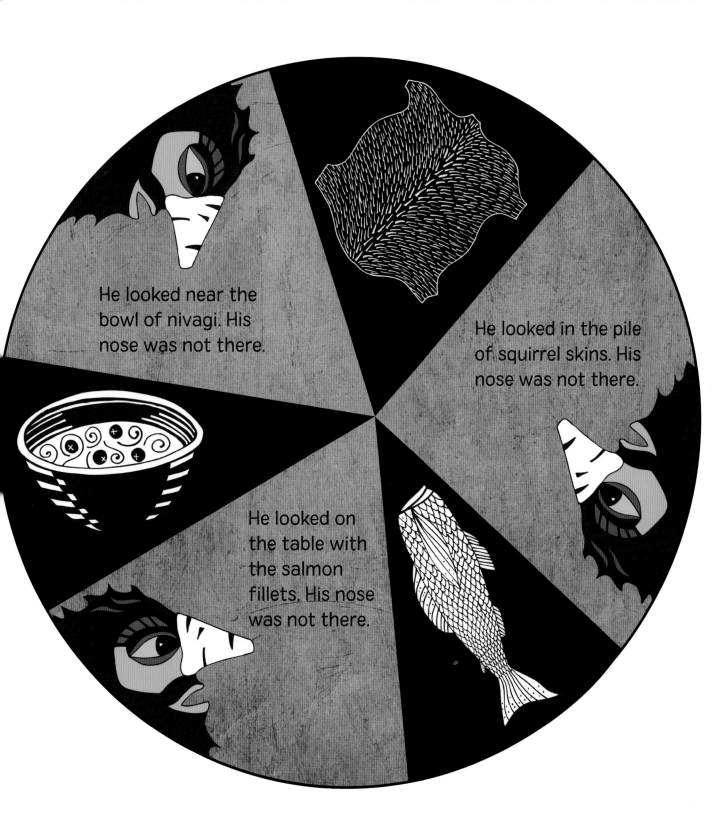

He looked near the bowl of nivagi. His nose was not there.

He looked in the pile of squirrel skins. His nose was not there.

He looked on the table with the salmon fillets. His nose was not there.

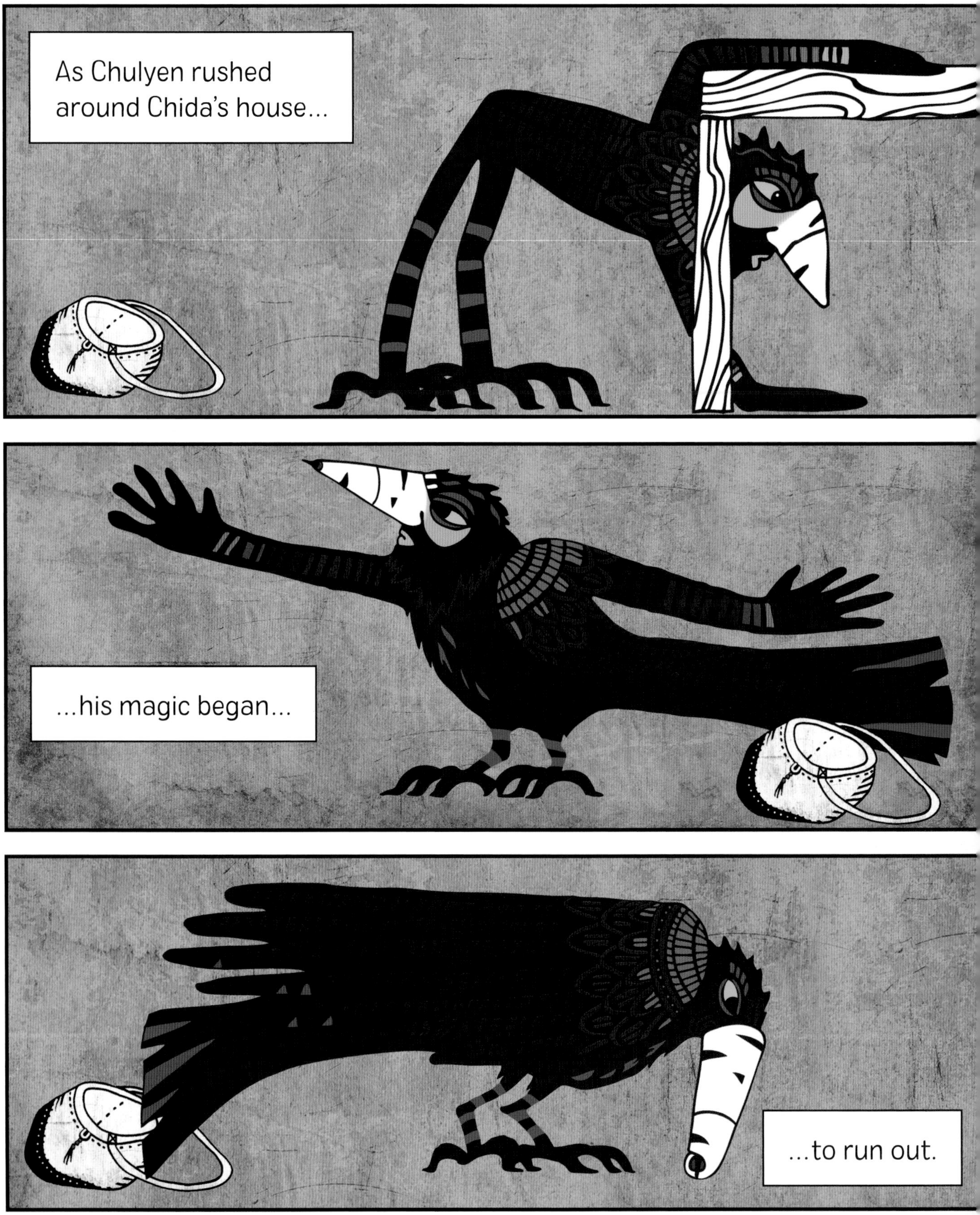
As Chulyen rushed around Chida's house...
...his magic began...
...to run out.

Where was his nose?

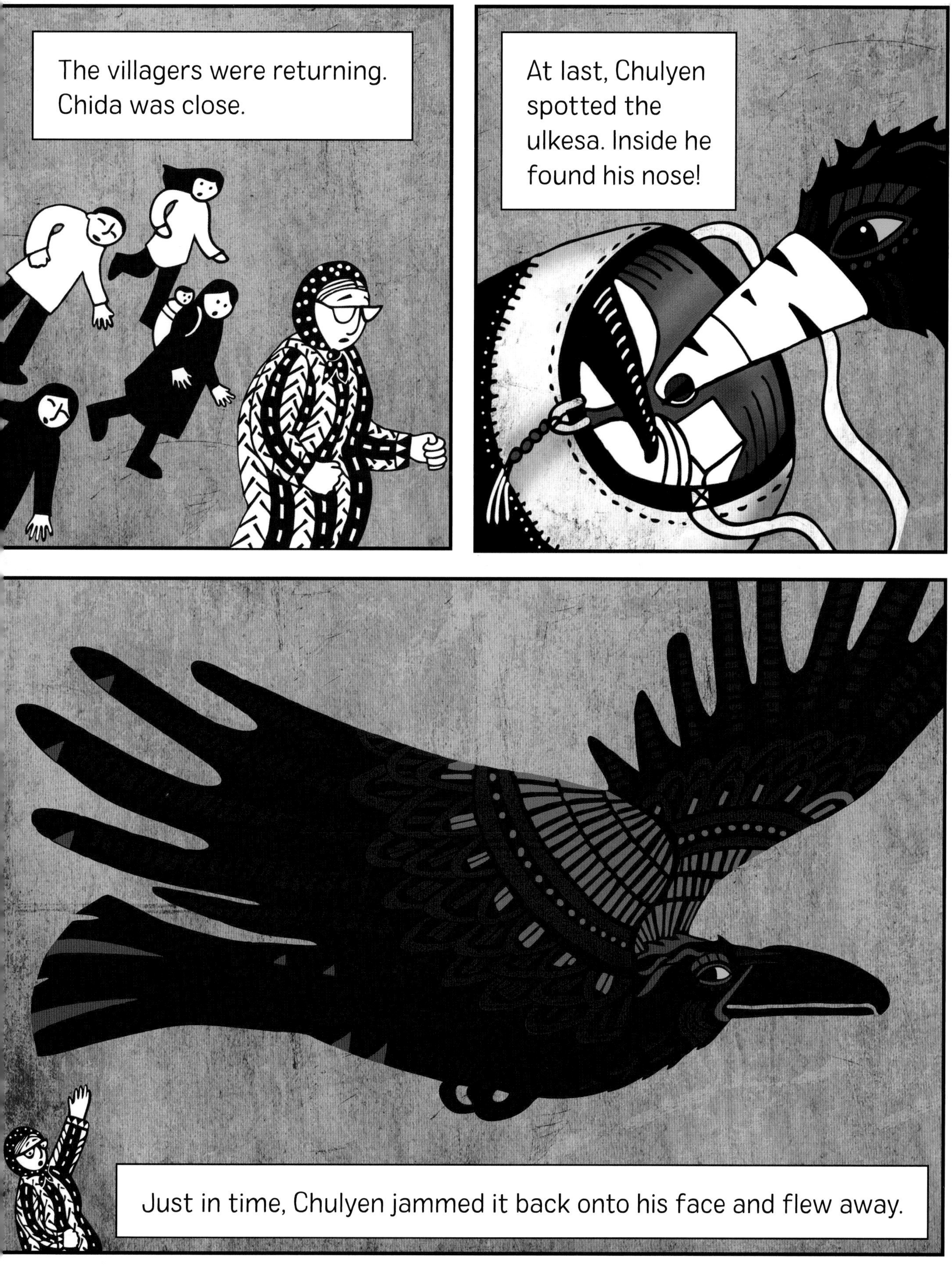
The villagers were returning. Chida was close.
At last, Chulyen spotted the ulkesa. Inside he found his nose!
Just in time, Chulyen jammed it back onto his face and flew away.

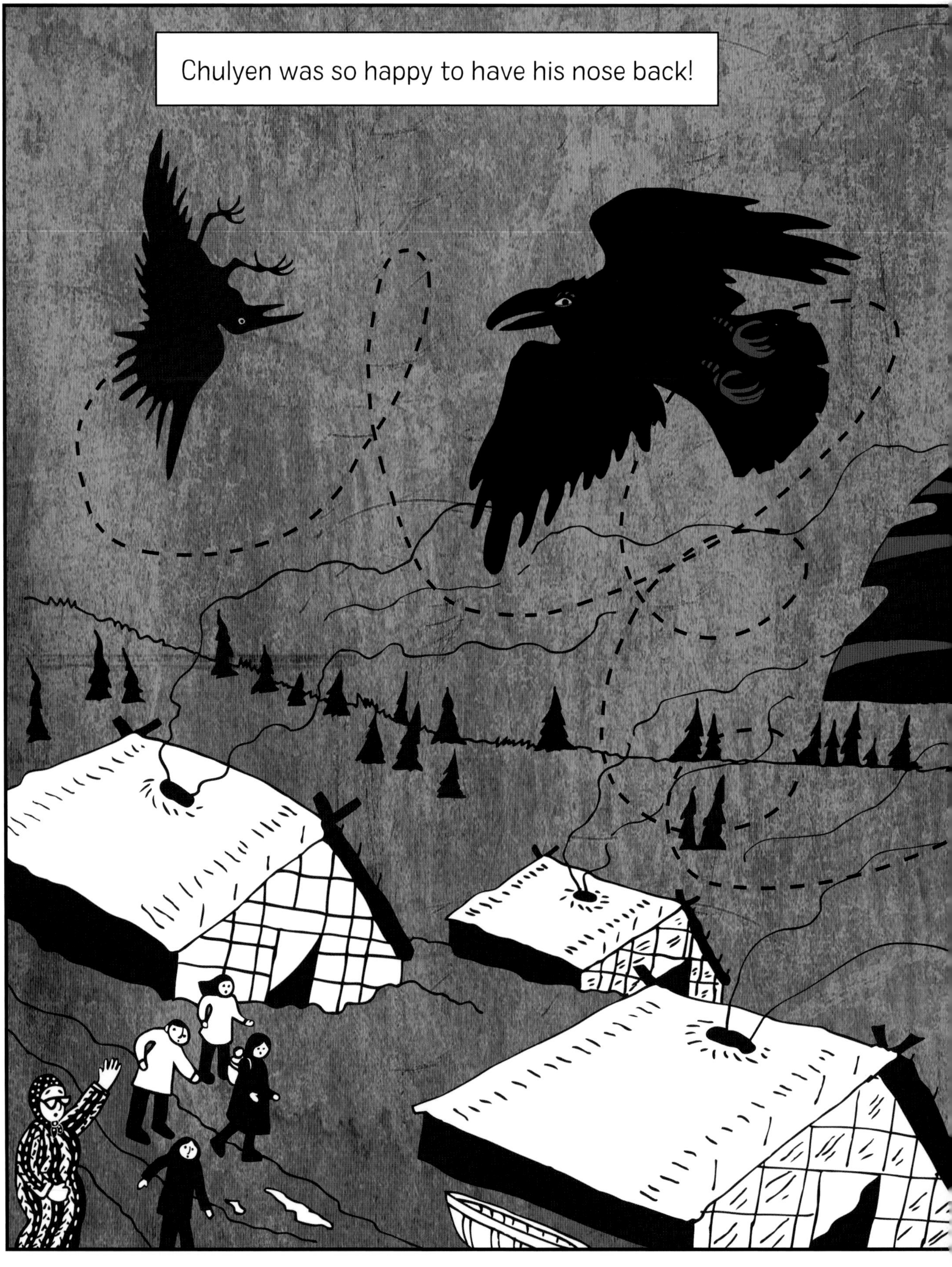
Chulyen was so happy to have his nose back!

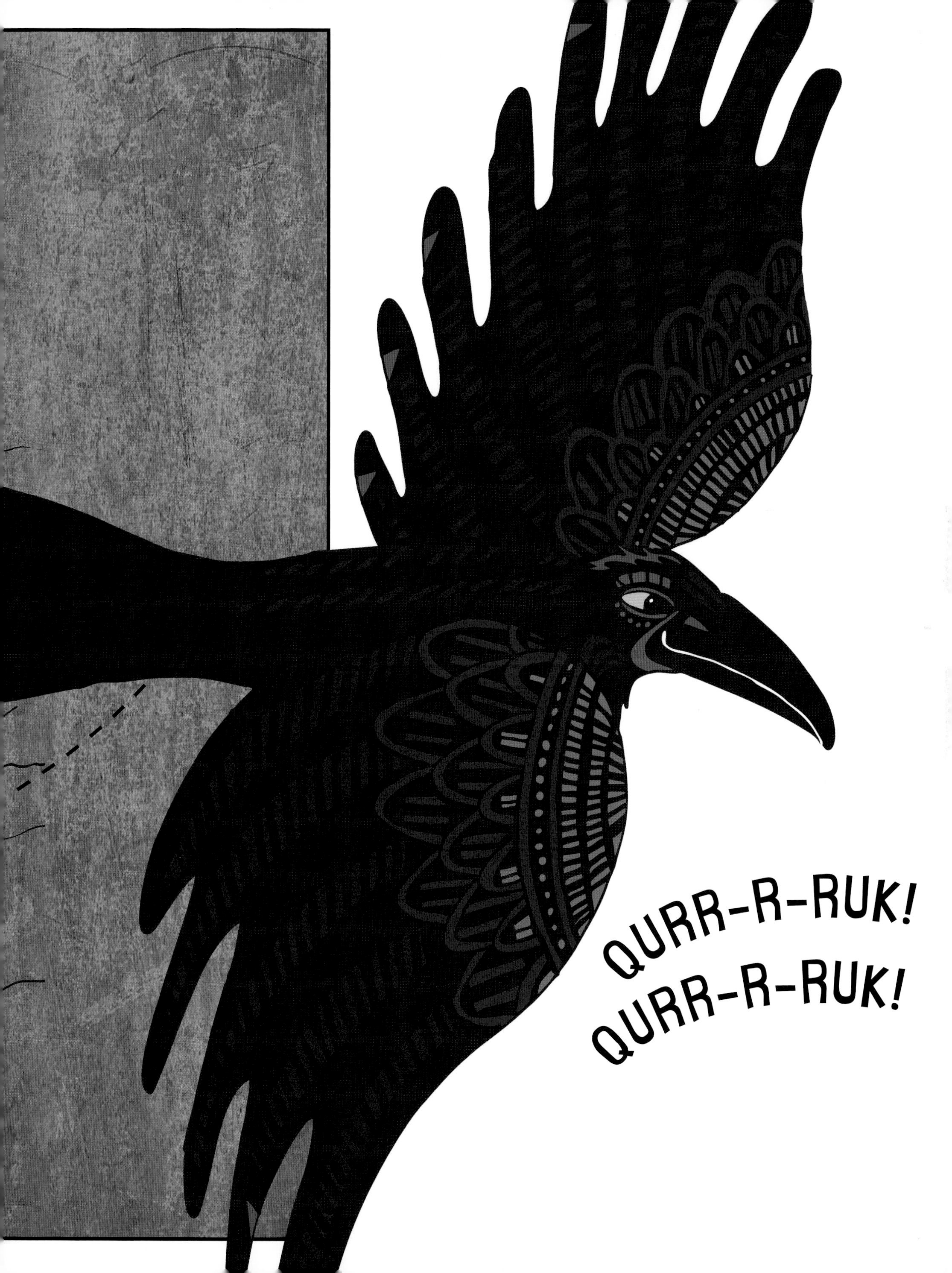
QURR-R-RUK!
QURR-R-RUK!

Well, Chulyen got his nose back, but if you look carefully you will notice something a little different. It had become soft and worn from Chida's use. Because he was hurrying, Chulyen did not notice. And because of his rush, he jammed it back on without care.

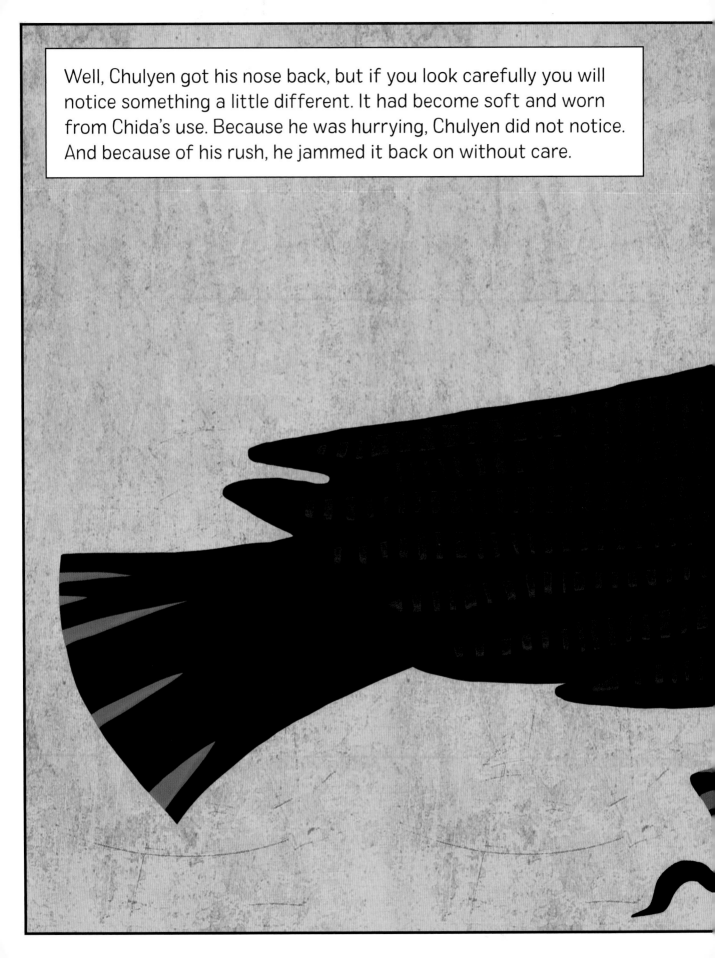

This is why Chulyen has a crooked nose.

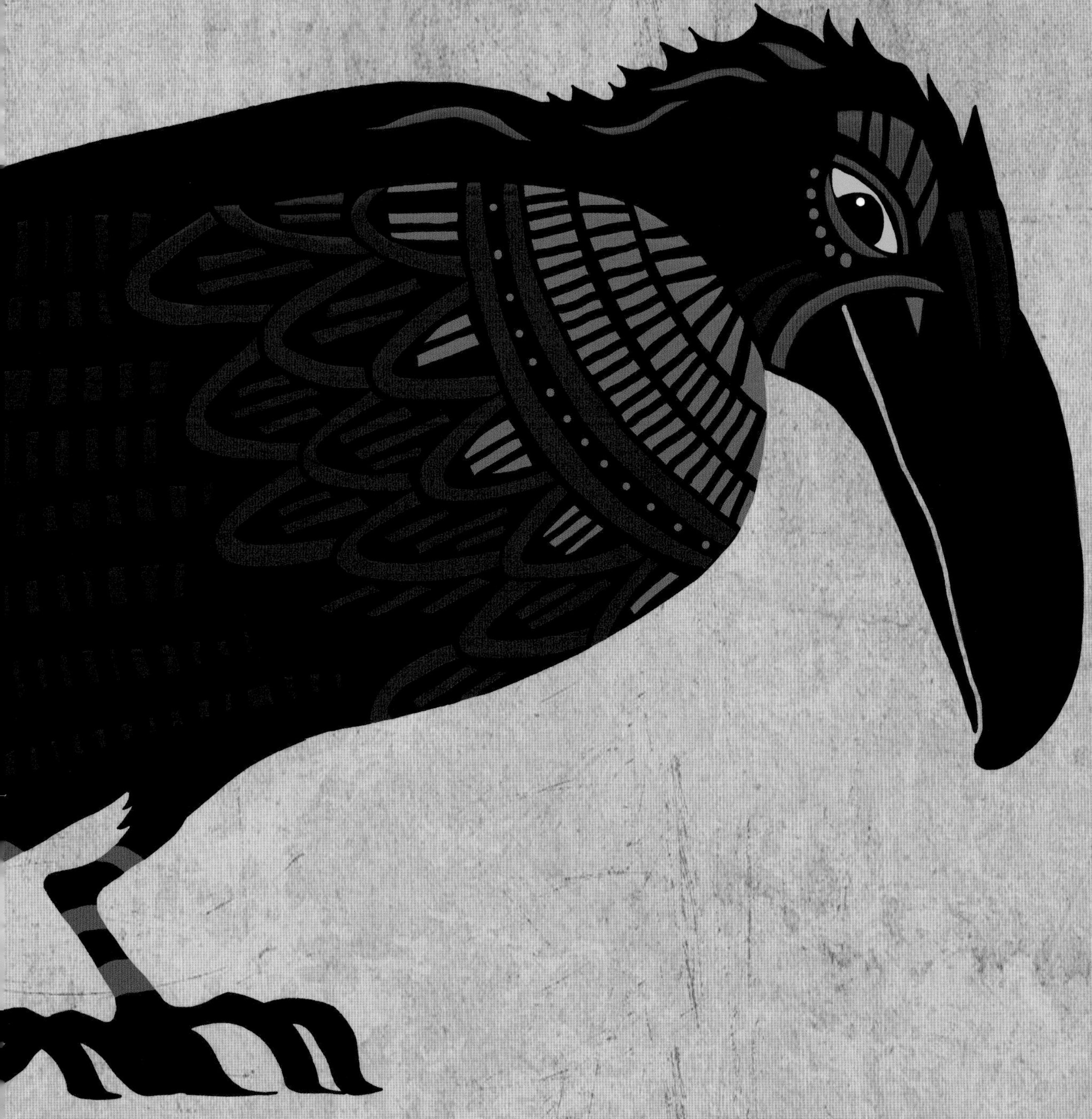

"It is always best to take our time and do things right. We may not get a chance to fix our mistakes," said Grandmother. "Just look at Chulyen—he still lives with a crooked nose."

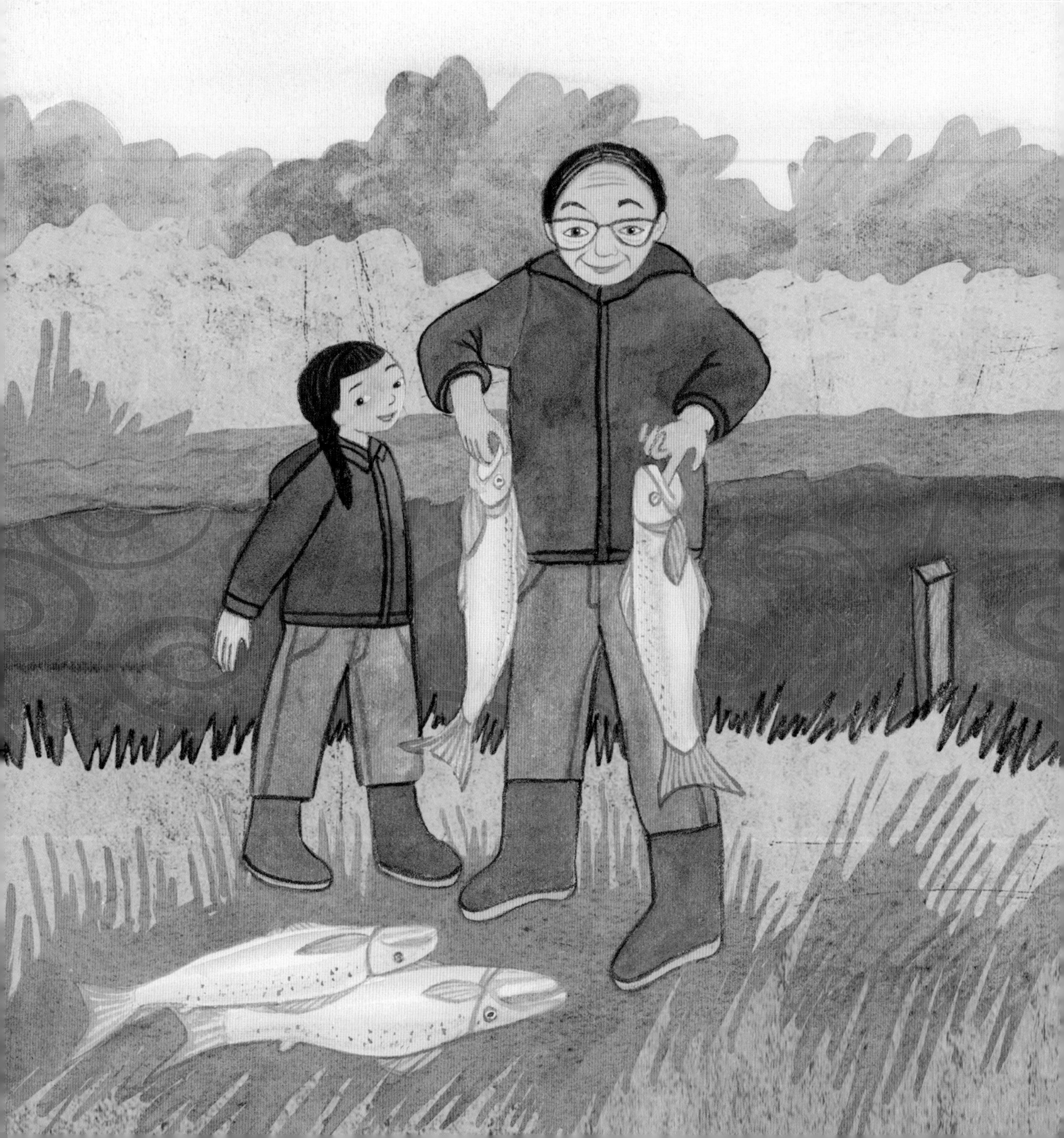

Dach' qidyuq. And that is what happened.

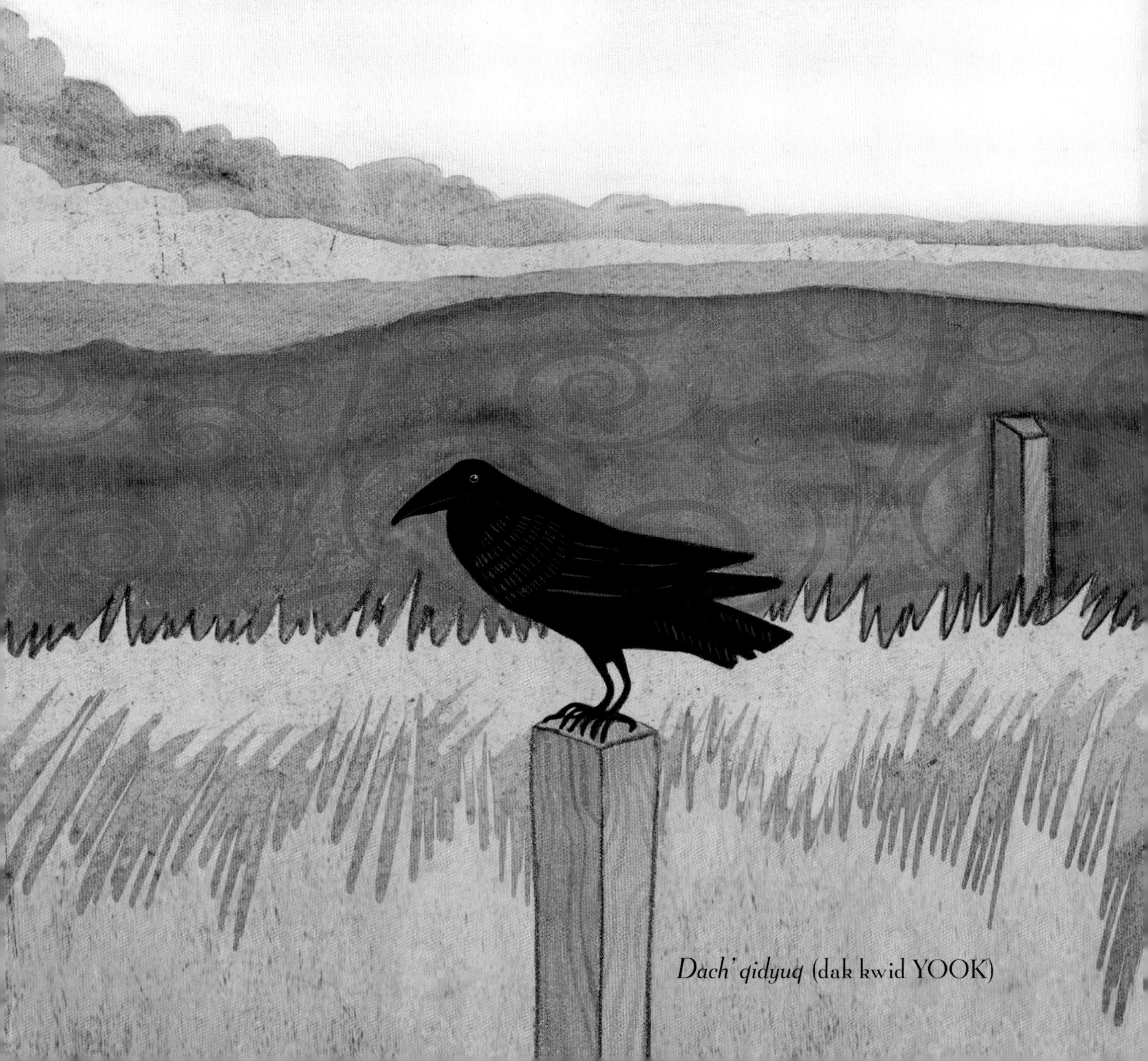

Dach' qidyuq (dak kwid YOOK)

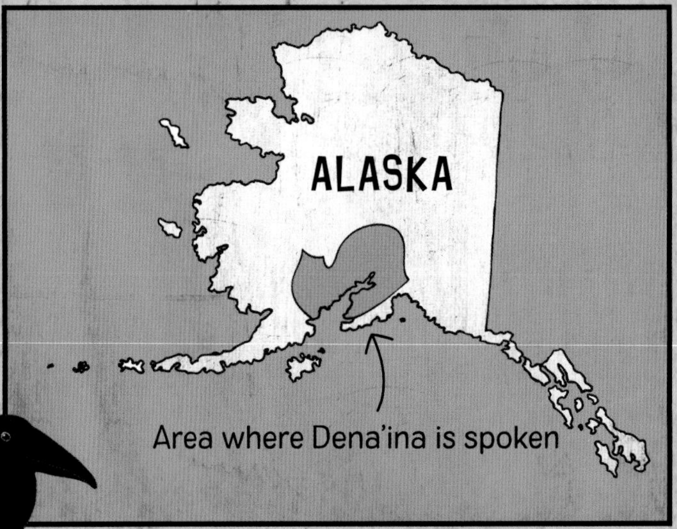
ALASKA
Area where Dena'ina is spoken

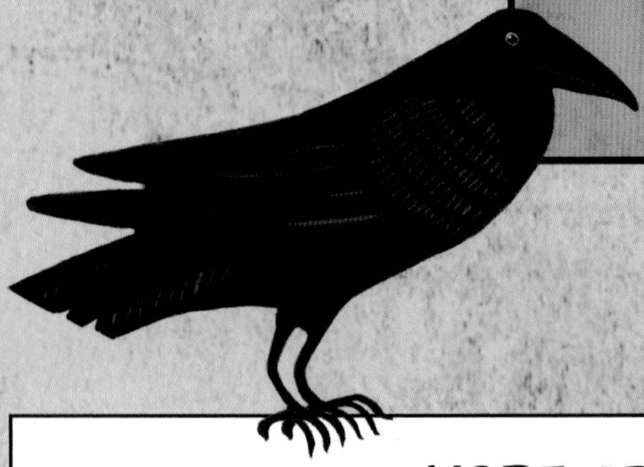

MORE ABOUT ALASKAN DENA'INA STORIES

The Dena'ina are an Athabascan language Native people that, to this day, live in the southern part of Alaska, mostly around Cook Inlet. They are the only Athabascan tribe to have migrated and taken up residence at a coastal location.

Their stories were often told to remind or teach their children how to behave. They discuss difficulties the people dealt with. Some are more historic in nature. They all tell something about the culture of the Dena'ina. The story of Chulyen's crooked nose is a teaching story.

Raven, prominent in the Dena'ina story lore as the trickster, often committed naughty and sometimes foolish acts. Like many animals in the Dena'ina stories, he had special powers that enabled him to do fantastical things.

Dena'ina homes were often built on hillsides, away from the shoreline. This made surprise attacks from enemies difficult. Squirrel skins were important to the people. Dena'ina women would climb a nearby mountain in the fall and spend several weeks trapping the arctic ground squirrel, also called the "parka squirrel." They made beautiful, warm blankets and parkas from the skins. Salmon, an essential food of the Dena'ina, was smoked to preserve it. The salmon was made into a kind of jerky that was eaten throughout the winter.

We use Dena'ina words where appropriate to remind us of the Dena'ina origins of the story, or *sukdu*. Dena'ina stories throughout time have ended with *dach' qidyuq*, meaning "and that is what happened..."

Chin'an. Thank you.

Barbara J. Atwater and Ethan J. Atwater
Anchorage, Alaska

DENA'INA GLOSSARY

Chida (CHEE da): grandma or old woman.

Chin'an (chi NUN): thank you.

Chulyen (CHOOL yen): raven.

Dach' qidyuq (dak kwid YOOK): And that is what happened.

K'eduzhizha (kuh ed UZH ee ZHA): Mouth, snout, or beak.
The traditional use of "nose" in this story is a personification
of the raven.

Nivagi (ni VAH gi): a favorite dish made with a mixture of fresh
berries and bound together with a creamed mixture of shortening,
sugar, and water or milk.

Sukdu (SOOK du): story.

Ulkesa (ul KEE suh): a small sewing bag
that women carried like a purse.

Yada di? (ya da DEE): What is it?

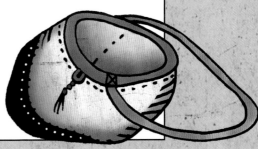

FURTHER READING

Atwater, Barbara J. *Walter's Story; Pedro Bay, Alaska - Past,
Present and Distant Memories*. Anchorage: Publication
Consultants, 2012.

Johnson, Walter. James Kari, ed. *I'll Tell You a Story (Sukdu
Nel Nuheghelnek); Stories I Recall from Growing up on
Iliamna Lake*. Fairbanks: Alaska Native Language Center,
University of Alaska Fairbanks, 2004.

Jones, Suzi, James A Fall, and Aaron Leggett, eds. *Dena'inaq'
Huch'ulyeshi; The Den'ina Way of Living*. Fairbanks: Alaska
Native Language Center, University of Alaska Fairbanks, 2013.

Kari, James, ed. *Dena'ina Topical Dictionary*. Fairbanks: Alaska
Native Language Center, University of Alaska Fairbanks, 2013.

DEDICATION

To our great uncle Walter Johnson who told us many stories, including this one. Whenever he told us a story he would say, "Now you go and tell this story in your own way." We have taken this both as permission and as a directive. *Chin'an*, thank you, Uncle Walter, for sharing this with us. We now share it with others.

How Raven Got His Crooked Nose
Text © 2018 by Barbara J. Atwater and Ethan J. Atwater
Illustrations © 2018 by Mindy Dwyer

Edited by Michelle McCann

All rights reserved. No part of this book may be reproduced or transmitted in any form or by any means, electronic or mechanical, including photocopying, recording, or by any information storage and retrieval system, without written permission of the publisher.

Library of Congress Cataloging-in-Publication Data is available

ISBN 9781513260952 (hardcover)
ISBN 9781513260969 (ebook)

Printed in China

Published by Alaska Northwest Books®
An imprint of

GRAPHIC ARTS
BOOKS®

GraphicArtsBooks.com

Graphic Arts Books
Publishing Director: Jennifer Newens
Marketing Manager: Angela Zbornik
Editor: Olivia Ngai
Design & Production: Rachel Lopez Metzger

BARBARA JACKO ATWATER is the daughter of George and Dolly (Foss) Jacko and was raised in the village of Pedro Bay, Alaska. Her great uncle, respected Dena'ina elder Walter Johnson, told her many Dena'ina fables, including the story of Chulyen the Raven, that she felt needed to be shared. An avid gardener and retired teacher, Barbara lives with her husband, Steve, in Anchorage, Alaska. Her favorite children's book is *Runaway Bunny*, by Margaret Wise Brown.

ETHAN JACKO ATWATER is the son of Steve and Barbara Jacko Atwater and was also raised in Pedro Bay. As a lover of stories, he enjoyed listening to his great, great uncle's fables and learning about the Dena'ina people and his culture in this way. Ethan lives in Anchorage, where he attends the University of Alaska Anchorage and works in a bookstore. His favorite children's book is *Where the Wild Things Are*, by Maurice Sendak.

How Raven Got His Crooked Nose is their first book for children.

MINDY DWYER is an illustrator and author of several Alaska-inspired books, including *Aurora, A Tale of the Northern Lights* and *The Salmon Princess*. Her favorite stories have always been the fairy tales, where a kind of magic still dances in the shadows from an ancient world. She and her family spent many happy years on top of a mountain in Alaska before they ran away with the circus and landed in Port Townsend, Washington. Mindy's favorite children's book is *Frederick*, by Leo Lionni.